RUTH
BY LAKE AND PRAIRIE

TRUE STORIES OF EARLY NAPERVILLE, ILLINOIS

The Telegraph's Route

N

Lake Ontario

Buffalo, New York

Dunkirk

Ashtabula

Lake Erie

Cleveland

Detroit

Mackinac Island

Lake Huron

Michigan

Manitou Islands

Lake Michigan

Fort Dearborn

Naper's Settlement

Wisconsin

Illinois

Indiana

Ohio

Pennsylvania

RUTH
BY LAKE AND PRAIRIE
TRUE STORIES OF EARLY NAPERVILLE, ILLINOIS

KATHARINE KENDZY GINGOLD

A
GNU VENTURES COMPANY
PUBLICATION
Naperville, IL

ISBN-13 978–0-9792419–0-1
ISBN-10 0–9792419–0-1

Printed in the U.S.A.

www.GnuVentures.net

CONTENTS

PREFACE

R uth Eliza Murray was a real girl. She truly did live in Ashtabula, Ohio with her family until they all moved with Uncle Joe out to Illinois to settle down near the DuPage River. No film crew documented the trip. There are no photographs, no diaries, no newspaper accounts. Years later, reporters interviewed the few settlers still living to record their memories, and some families have passed down old stories, but very little information exists about the founding of Naper's Settlement.

Recreating Ruth's story meant being a detective. Even simple facts had to be checked and rechecked. How old was Ruth in 1831? Was her birthday before or after the July trip? Is there a birth record or a gravestone to prove it? How did she look? Was she smart? Funny? Nice?

Tiny clues helped to build Ruth's character: Her parents were Scottish and Irish, two nationalities that have the highest incidence of red hair. Ruth didn't marry as young as her sisters did. Maybe she felt less attractive. Ruth's older sister, Sally Ann, named a daughter after Ruth, so there must have been affection between them. Little by little, Ruth Eliza Murray came alive again.

The same detective work was done for each of the people in the story, as well as for the ship they traveled on and the cities they visited. Woven around the historical facts is the imagined day-to-day life of the twelve-year-old girl who experienced this journey.

Knowing our history helps us understand our own place in it. Ruth's grandfather fought in the Revolutionary War. After Ruth settled on the DuPage River, forty years would pass before Laura Ingalls Wilder lived in her little house on the prairie. And when Wilder died, Disneyland had already been delighting children for years.

It's not so far after all to reach back through the years and shake hands with a girl from 1831, when our town, Naperville, was born.

ACKNOWLEDGEMENTS

What I thought would be just a fresh retelling of a traditional story turned into a major research project that continues even now. Gathering up the facts—known, forgotten and new—proved time-consuming, but absolutely fascinating. Many, many people contributed information generously and enthusiastically. This book would never have taken shape without them, and I thank them from the bottom of my heart.

For their encouragement and expert knowledge, special thanks must go to Susan Degges and Bryan Ogg of the Naperville Heritage Society, Louise Legeza of the Geneva Public Library in Ohio, Warrenville City Historian Leone Schmidt, and local Naperville historians Peg Yonker, Mary Lou Wehrli, and Madeline and Eldon Hatch.

I am also grateful for the helpful staff people at the Naperville Public Library, the DuPage County Historical Museum, the Plainfield Public Library, the Chicago History Museum, and the Wheaton Public Library.

For facts about the early days on the Great Lakes, I

am indebted to Dr. Theodore Karamanski, Walter Lewis, Fred Neushel and other members of the Chicago Maritime Society.

Through the Internet I developed online relationships with many of the descendents of the settlers who shared the results of their genealogical research with me. Thank you to Jackie Doeden (of Cordelia Murray's family); Jean Bellinger, Nancy Bruce Crilly and Gary Ward (of the Sisson Family); Murray Shattuck, Sr. and Murray and Lisa Shattuck, Jr. (of Ruth Murray's family); and Chris Marceille (of Almeda Landon's family).

I am especially thankful to Kim Winters and Sara TerMaat for their writing advice and professional insight. Also special thanks to my critical readers: Caroline and Mary, Mary and Allie, Mr. Horner's PI+ class, Jacob, Keaton and Sarah.

I'd also like to thank my parents, Ken and Arlene Kendzy, for their life-long encouragement and patience. Thanks also to my son James and daughter Emily, for their assumption that "mom's writing a book" is the ordinary sort of thing one deals with.

Finally, I owe a huge debt of gratitude to my husband, Don, who did everything in his power to make my road smoother. He pushed, pulled and never let me give up.

RUTH
BY LAKE AND PRAIRIE
TRUE STORIES OF EARLY NAPERVILLE, ILLINOIS

CHAPTER 1

SETTING SAIL FROM ASHTABULA

Clinging to the edge of the great gray expanse of Lake Erie, the little two-masted schooner bobbed up and down as Ruth shuffled sideways across the narrow gangplank. Although the gangplank was barely wide enough for one person, she had watched sailors run confidently over the swaying board from dock to ship. Ruth doubted whether she would make it across without disaster. Leading the way, Cordelia tugged eagerly at Ruth's hand while Gran hung back, clutching at Ruth's other arm. Pulled between them, Ruth teetered along the plank, trying not to look down at the choppy water below.

Uncle Joe came to the edge of the ship, reaching out to help them across. Finally stepping safely on the wooden deck, Ruth glanced behind her. Her brothers were still on the pier with Mother, hearing last minute instructions from Daidí. In the rush to board, Ruth had missed bidding Daidí farewell, and now, burdened with baggage, a little sister, and Gran, she couldn't even lift a hand to wave. Daidí usually saved an extra smile for her, which made being the middle and most ordinary child more bearable, but apparently he'd forgotten in all the bustle.

Schooner
A sailing vessel with at least two masts, the shorter one in front.

Ruth bit back her disappointment and guided her charges away from the gangplank and through the crowd of passengers.

Cordelia clamored to look about, but with an eye on the threatening clouds overhead, Gran insisted on making for the cabin. Ruth patiently shushed the six-year-old's protests. Seeing to Gran's comfort was Ruth's responsibility now that Sally Ann was married and had her own family to look after.

"You'll have all the way from Ohio to Illinois to explore the *Telegraph*," Ruth assured Cordelia.

Looking back to the dock one last time, Ruth saw Sally Ann wiping away tears with the tail of the baby's blanket as her husband Henry kissed them both goodbye. Staying behind to drive the cattle overland, Henry and Daidí planned to meet up with the ship at Fort Dearborn. That left teenaged Ned as the man of the family during the voyage, but calling Ned a man always made Ruth giggle since he was only a few years older than she. Even now, she could hear his self-important voice upraised as he ordered their younger brother Amos on board.

As Ruth neared the cabin with Gran and Cordelia in tow, two small bodies tumbled out of the doorway. Aunt

Betsy followed wearing her usual merry grin.

"Why, there you are!" she exclaimed. "I've got a lovely seat all ready for you, Granny Naper! Be a love and watch the boys a moment, will you, Ruth? Then I can get Gran settled. Give me your sack, Gran, and watch your step there."

The little boys and Cordelia hugged joyfully, bouncing up and down, as if they hadn't seen each other nearly every day of their lives. Ruth let her bags and baskets slip to the deck and stretched her sore muscles. A gust of wind knocked her bonnet back, the ribbon catching at her throat. She turned to see if the others had come aboard yet. Yes, there they were, gingerly stepping across the gangplank: Mother, then both boys, and behind them, arms loaded with parcels, was—

"Daidí!" Ruth grabbed the children and gave them a little shake. "Stay right here! Stay with the luggage!" She squirmed through the crowd to where her father was handing his packages over to Uncle Joe. He turned and hugged her hard. "I couldn't let the ship sail off without saying goodbye to my wee Cailín.

Gangplank
The board used as a ramp between a ship and the dock.

"No tears, now. Your mother and sisters will be needing your help more

3

than ever. But they're the lucky ones!" He smiled and chucked her under the chin. "I'll have no one to tell the old tales to until we meet again in Fort Dearborn. Henry and the oxen won't listen as they ought, and they never laugh in the right places like my wee Cailín does!"

Two sailors started to drag the gangplank back onto the deck. Uncle Joe clapped Daidí on the back. "You'd best be off, John!" As quick as a sailor, Daidí climbed over the rail and leaped to the dock. The anchor was raised and as the ship slowly pulled away, Daidí took off his hat and waved it overhead. Mother didn't wave, but she blinked as if her eyes stung. Sally Ann wailed as loud as the baby she clutched against her chest, and Mother spoke to her in a low voice that Ruth only barely heard.

"You don't want your husband to remember you like this. Smile for him! It's the last he'll see of you for weeks." Sally hiccupped and straightened her shoulders, smiling so brightly that Henry would be sure to see her over the widening gap between the ship and shore.

Everyone jostled to get a last look at their little town of Ashtabula. Ruth suddenly remembered she had left Cordelia and the Naper boys by the cabin, and threaded her way back. They were no longer jumping, but huddled together solemnly in the forest of trousers and gowns. Ruth lifted Cordelia up for a last look. "Say 'farewell' to Ohio, Cordelia! We're off to a new home in Illinois." Cordelia waved as the two little boys pulled at Ruth's skirt, demanding to see, too.

4

Aunt Betsy joined them, hoisting a boy up on each hip. "So, we're on our way! Gran didn't want to come up to see us cast off. She said her goodbyes yesterday." Ruth nodded, remembering how they had stopped at the cemetery where the grass was only just beginning to cover the bare earth of Grandfather's grave. She could almost see the cemetery from here, high atop one of the green and overgrown bluffs that loomed over the harbor village.

As the familiar shore slipped away behind them, Ruth suddenly had a vision of Maimeó and Daideó, her Murray grandparents, standing just like this at the rail of another ship as Ireland faded into the distance. Ruth heard sniffling in the crowd behind her and felt an answering lump rise in her throat. In this year of 1831 dear Ashtabula finally felt civilized, like a community instead of a fur-traders' camp. Now they would be starting all over again.

Ruth glanced sideways at the dark little woman beside her. Although it was a weak sun breaking over the bluffs, Ruth could see there were no tears in her eyes. "Will you miss Ashtabula, Aunt Betsy?" she asked.

Betsy smiled and shrugged. "Oh, some things. But we're all going together—your Ma and Sally Ann and your Gran. This isn't the first time I've left a home behind. Now my home is wherever these little imps are." She planted loud kisses on each tousled head "Did I say 'little'? I feel like I'm carrying a couple of millstones!" She set the children down with a laugh. "Why don't you leave Cordelia with me and bring the rest of those bags down to the cabin. You can look in on Gran while you're there."

Ruth gathered up the baskets and sacks that were still lying on the deck and stepped down into the cabin. Two tall men could easily span its width with arms outstretched and the narrow chamber was made smaller by a table and a couple of benches. A rope down the center of the room held a curtain, now pulled back to make the most of the space. Later, it would separate the men's sleeping area from the women's.

Granny Naper was enthroned at the far end on a small chest padded with blankets from the family's bedrolls. She looked up sharply from her knitting. "We've cast off then?"

"Yes, Gran. I've brought the last of the bags."

"Well, bring them here. Move Betsy's bundle over a bit." Ruth did as she was told, and then hovered near the door, trying to catch a glimpse outside. She longed to be up on deck with the others, watching the wild scenery as the little schooner sped along the coast.

Most often it was Ruth that Mother asked to sit with the old ones or mind the children. Ruth obeyed out of habit, and her friendly nature usually made the chore pleasant. "But still," Ruth thought resentfully, "why am I always the one left behind?" Distracted by her restlessness, Gran looked up again, this time with a smile.

"I'm perfectly comfortable here, Ruth Eliza, and I've plenty of wool. Go on up. I'm sure it's a fine sight." Ruth needed no other urging.

On deck, the passengers who had just boarded gathered on the land side of the ship. Some gripped the rail with white-knuckled fingers while others chattered excitedly about the journey. The families from Buffalo and Dunkirk were already experienced travelers after the trip from New York and stood back to watch the newcomers with superior smiles.

Aunt Betsy was standing with Mother, Sally Ann, and an elegantly dressed woman Ruth recognized as Aunt Almeda, who had moved to Dunkirk several years ago. Cordelia was happily bossing all the little cousins as they played around the feet of their mothers, but Ruth noticed Amos edging away, his eye on several older boys who must have boarded earlier in the run.

Uncle Jack stood at the ship's wheel with Uncle Joe and Ned on either side of him. Although the *Telegraph* belonged to both uncles, Ruth knew Uncle Jack was her captain. Ned was probably just being a pest, but seeing the three standing together was a shock. Ruth had never realized before how much Ned looked like his Naper uncles rather than their father, broad across the shoulders with the same thick neck and big hands. Daidí was strong and ruddy from a lifetime of farming, but he didn't take up nearly as much space as these Naper men.

As Ruth's gaze moved across the ship, she was

suddenly aware that someone was watching her as well, a girl around her own age wearing a dress of store-bought calico. The dress was not new, but the blue print was only gently faded and fit her slender frame perfectly. The pure oval of her face and the girl's dark-rimmed eyes reminded Ruth of a book engraving she once saw of a medieval queen.

Calico

A cheap, cotton fabric with a printed design, originally imported from Calicut, India.

Along with some other passengers, the girl perched on the wooden box that framed a great square hole in the deck. With the cargo stored away and the door banged to, the ledge around the cargo hold served as a bench. From her seat, the girl smiled in a friendly fashion, and Ruth moved a little closer. Once Ruth was near, though, her tongue became shy. Not that it mattered. The girl continued to smile and soon burst into enthusiastic conversation.

"I am so glad you boarded! There are only mothers and babies on this ship. Well, and Mary, but she is practically a mother already, raising her father's second family. She is simply not sympathetic. But I can tell already that you, you are a fellow soul!" She sat back on the rim of the cargo hold, beaming.

Ruth felt that some answer was expected of her, but not knowing what a "fellow soul" was, she couldn't think of an appropriate response. The girl didn't seem to notice. "I know who you are—you're Ruth Murray. I know because your aunt told me you would be boarding in Ashtabula. You're prettier than she said you were—" She clapped her hand over her mouth, horrified.

Ruth brushed away the girl's apologies. It was more surprising to hear that this girl thought her slightly pretty than to know that Aunt Almeda had described her as plain. Mother always said that Sally Ann, with her black Irish eyes and creamy skin, was pretty. This girl with the glossy brown braids was pretty. But Ruth never considered her sandy hair and freckles pretty. She drew a little nearer.

"I'm afraid I don't know who you are."

The girl extended her hand gracefully. "I am Mariah Sisson. We are from New York, and we also lived in Indiana, but I have never been to Illinois before."

"I've never been anywhere besides Ashtabula, Ohio," Ruth replied.

Mariah patted the space beside her, inviting Ruth to sit. "This is the first time I've ever been on a ship. I thought it would be more, oh! more *liberating* to journey by ship. But the little ones need so much looking after, and the adults are mostly ill. And now it's so crowded." She gestured across the deck where passengers were wedged tightly among wagon boxes, oxen yokes, and

9

other bulky odds and ends.

"But the sailors are very interesting! I've never known more *colorful* language. Mama almost *faints* when she hears their cursing!" She giggled and nodded towards a dark-haired woman who was holding her wind-blown bonnet down with one hand and a small child close with the other. The woman had tied her gown as loose as could be, but it was obvious she was close to her lying-in time.

The sun retreated behind the clouds and Ruth shivered a little. It was chilly for a June day. Watching the rocky shore slide past, Ruth thought the forests looked dark and forbidding even though the trees were not yet fully leafed out. She could see no sunny meadows, no flowers, and no signs of civilization.

"Was it like this from Dunkirk to Ashtabula? All forest?" Ruth asked.

"Oh no! Well, that is, there were lots of forests, but also towns and trading posts. And Indian villages. At one, we dropped anchor, and there were all these little children playing in the shallows, naked as newborns, and this old squaw was in a canoe, circling the ship, with a horrid scar that started above her eye and..."

"Ruth! Ruth Eliza!"

Mariah's story had caught her up so completely that Ruth hadn't even noticed Mother standing beside her until she heard her name. Both girls jumped to their feet. Mrs. Sisson and the aunts were with Mother, as well as some women Ruth did not know.

"Well, I see you and Mariah have already met!" Mother turned to the ladies. "This is my middle daughter, Ruth." Ruth bobbed a shy curtsey. "I'm going in to Granny Naper, so please keep Amos and Cordelia from falling overboard while I'm gone."

Canoe

A boat made of birch bark so lightweight, a squaw, or American Indian wife, could paddle it herself.

"Yes'm." Ruth took a step towards Amos, who was showing Cordelia and a small plump girl something in his hand that was apparently rather disgusting, to judge by the girls' faces. Ruth glanced back at Mariah with a questioning look.

"I'll come along—that's my little sister with them."

Together, Ruth and Mariah picked their way across to where half dozen children sang a handclap rhyme. Amos carefully rewrapped whatever it was in his handkerchief and tucked it away. "I reckon he brought that old mouse skull along," Ruth smiled to herself. With both of her charges safely in view as they waited to join the game, Ruth eagerly returned to Mariah's story. "Tell me some more about the Indian village."

Flattered, Mariah began again. The children lost interest in their handclap, drawn by her dramatic storytelling. They inched closer and closer until they were actually pressing against the older girls or sitting on their knees.

In her familiar role as listener, Ruth compared Mariah's tale-telling to Daidí's. While she was painfully aware that her own thoughts were of the plain, homespun sort, the flights of fancy created by others always delighted her. Ruth humbly admired good storytelling. And if the truth were told, she secretly prided herself on her judgment of the storyteller.

Suspecting that Mariah overly exaggerated some details, Ruth nevertheless appreciated the excitement they added, and the morning sped away as fast as their little schooner. The menfolk were called to the table for their dinner, and Ruth heard her own stomach answer the summons. Without enough room in the tiny cabin, the children wouldn't be fed until the last shift. Now she regretted being too excited to eat before boarding!

When the men returned to lean against the rails and try to smoke their pipes in the steady breeze, the women went in to their

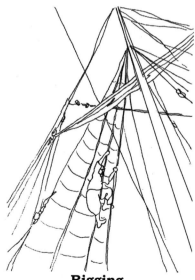

Rigging
The ropes that control the sails on a ship.

12

dinner. All, that is, save one, who hadn't moved all morning. She cowered against a stack of wagon boxes lashed to the deck, their wheels removed and hung in the rigging overhead. Ruth recognized the woman as Mrs. Graves from the tavern in the lower village at Ashtabula. Mrs. Graves had boarded the ship in great distress and was still clutching her small daughter close with trembling hands. Louisa, her nearly grown stepdaughter, came by to call her to dinner, but obviously found it a tiresome duty. After Mrs. Graves refused her halfhearted invitation, Louisa sassed back in a tone Ruth would never have dared use. Mrs. Graves, however, just turned her face away. Laughing at her stepmother's anxiety, Louisa threw out a last sarcastic remark and flounced off.

The scene playing out on deck interested Ruth more than Mariah's tale. Ruth knew right away that badgering Mrs. Graves would only deepen her stubbornness. "You keep poking a stick at an animal and they just back up farther out of reach," she thought, shaking her head.

Mariah started a new story for the children about a very unlikely conversation between a rabbit and a bear. Seeing Cordelia entranced and even Amos practically climbing in Mariah's lap to catch every word, Ruth felt able to leave them for a moment.

She walked over slowly to Mrs. Graves and sat down near her. Mrs. Graves didn't move, but the little girl looked up at Ruth with frightened eyes.

"How d'ye do, Mrs. Graves. Remember me, Ruth Murray? Your little girl looks hungry and it's time for dinner. I'll take her in, if you like, with my little sister. I'll look after her real well." There was no answer.

"Mrs. Graves?" Ruth tried again, gently. The woman shook her head, refusing to look at her.

The girl whimpered. "Mama, I'm hungry." Slowly, the woman opened her eyes. Her gaze darted wildly around the ship, as if expecting to see threat of shipwreck at any moment, before resting on the white and pinched face of her little daughter. Finally, she lifted her gaze to meet Ruth's, as if realizing for the first time that someone was there.

Using the same voice that persuaded skittish horses into the barn, Ruth repeated her offer. Mrs. Graves gave a short nod and let Ruth draw the girl away. "I'll bring her right back, ma'am, after dinner." Mrs. Graves nodded again.

Firmly holding the child by the hand, Ruth rejoined the circle around Mariah. When the women finished their meal the children were called into the cabin. Although taken up once again with Sally Ann and her baby, Mother turned when Ruth passed by with Cordelia, Amos and the Graves girl. Their eyes met, and Mother gave an approving nod that made Ruth stand a little taller.

CHAPTER 2

LEARNING THE ROPES

As the children entered the ship's small cabin, a boiling kettle called out from the stubby iron stove in the back. Enthroned on her quilt-cushioned trunk, Granny Naper snored gently in reply. After all morning on the breezy deck, the stuffy air inside made Ruth's stomach churn and she didn't really feel like eating anymore. Ruth pushed her bonnet back and helped Lucy Graves loosen hers as well.

A tall girl was measuring tea into a teapot. "Come to the table, and I'll tell you newcomers how we do our chores on the *Telegraph*," she said without looking up.

More than two dozen children stood around the long table, shoulder to shoulder in the tight space. Most were Amos and Cordelia's age or even younger. Only a few boys looked to be around twelve like her, and there were none older save the girl with the teapot. Ned was grown up enough to

Iron Stove
Made of metal and hollow to burn wood inside, it radiates heat for warmth and has a cooking surface on top.

15

eat with the men, and Ruth suddenly realized her time eating with the children was nearly at an end as well.

Once the tall girl poured the boiling water from the kettle to the teapot, she looked up. "You little ones—when it's your turn, come into the cabin quietly and stand by the table. The rest of us will fetch dinner and clear away with everyone doing their share." She shot a stern glance at the newcomers, but Louisa Graves just rolled her eyes and snorted.

Mariah and two other girls were busily placing mugs on the table and handing out slabs of ship's biscuit and cold ham. Swallowing down the churning feeling inside her, Ruth instantly stepped away from the table. "What should I be doing?" she asked.

The tall girl waved a hand toward the teapot. "You can pour out while I put the tea caddy away."

As Ruth reached for a mug, she put a hand on the table to steady herself, but pulled it back quickly. "Someone spilled," she said.

Tea Caddy

A special small box to hold the loose leaves of expensive tea.

Mariah laughed. "Not exactly! We dampen the tablecloth to keep the mugs from sliding right off the edge when the ship rocks. It mostly works, but keep an eye out all the same!"

Once all the mugs were filled, without any help from Louisa, they

16

were handed around, each shared by two children. Already familiar with the routine, those from Dunkirk paired up automatically. Louisa reluctantly let her little sister Lucy share with her, and Amos paired up with Cordelia. Ruth supervised her young Naper cousins, sharing a mug with Georgie.

After the tall girl gave thanks, the children ate. The ham tasted just like home, but Ruth had never had ship's biscuit before. She tried to nibble a piece, but it was so hard she felt like a beaver gnawing on a tree trunk. Then Ruth noticed Mariah dipping her biscuit into her mug, softening it with the hot tea, and she tried the same. The biscuit was still pretty tasteless, but at least she could eat it and it didn't upset her stomach too much. Ruth dunked Georgie's biscuit as well, and put it in his chubby fist.

Alternating bites of biscuit with ham made for a tolerable meal, washed down with hot, weak tea. Ruth left half in the mug to cool for Georgie. Eager to get back outside, she joined the older girls in tidying up the cabin and sweeping up the few crumbs while the younger children made use of the chamber pot.

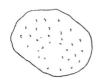

Ship's Biscuit
A cracker so hard and dry, it won't get moldy on long trips.

Two of the girls spent the entire meal whispering confidences to each other. Mariah said one was her sister Harriet and the other was Harriet's bosom friend Addie, but Ruth wasn't sure which was which. The whispering now dissolved into giggles, and finally they approached the tall girl, arm in arm.

"Mary, we think the new girls should take slops duty today. We already know how."

"Harriet, you're always trying to get out of your chores!" Mariah protested, but Mary just shrugged. Louisa quickly grabbed Lucy's hand and dragged her out the door, mumbling something about the little girl needing her mother. Ruth and Mariah exchanged glances as the door banged behind her. "Rude!" Mariah mouthed, and Ruth nodded in agreement.

Mary pointed out the crockery chamber pail to Ruth. "Make sure you dump it off the stern of the ship," she warned. "You have to go behind to dump it or the wind will toss it right back at you."

Ruth nodded, but then caught sight of the teapot. "Can I have what's left of the tea when I get back?" Mary just shrugged again, so Ruth poured out most of a mug-full, setting it on the stove to stay warm. Then she picked up the crock and with great concentration, carried it up the steps.

Chamber Pot
A portable bucket used as a toilet.

As the ship rolled from side to side, Ruth tried to sway the opposite way to keep the chamber pot level. She made her way safely to the back of the ship, the folks on deck only too anxious to make way for her, and made ready to toss the contents overboard.

"Keep a good grip, or you'll lose it!" Uncle Jack laughed from his position at the ship's wheel. But no such catastrophe occurred, and Ruth returned the pot to its accustomed place inside.

People drifted back into the cabin to get out of the wind, play cards, or put little ones down to rest. Ruth added some hot water from the kettle to the mug of tea on the stove before carefully climbing the stairs once more. She knelt in front of Mrs. Graves, holding the mug out to her. The older woman stared for a moment, and then shook her head, drawing even farther back.

Ship's Wheel
Connected by mechanics to the rudder, the wheel was used to steer the ship.

"It's a cup of tea, Mrs. Graves. It'll warm you up and settle your stomach. Your little girl Lucy had some, and she feels ever so much better. Try to drink a little."

Ruth was afraid the tea would be cold by the time she convinced Mrs. Graves, but before long, she was able to put the mug into the woman's hands. After a sip or two, Mrs. Graves' lips lost a little of their blue color.

If Aunt Betsy had brought the tea, she would be chattering away like a squirrel, but Ruth figured silence would better draw Mrs. Graves out of herself. Sitting quietly, Ruth let her gaze wander. Amos was teasing Cordelia and her new friends. Lucy was hovering on the edge of the group, too shy to join the other children. Presently, Mrs. Graves began to talk, and Ruth smiled to herself. She had figured right.

"I—I didn't know they could make tea on a boat. Thank you for bringing it to me. It's good." She offered only the ghost of a smile, but continued to talk.

"I don't know about boats at all. Mr. Graves never told me very much. It—it didn't look so small from the wharf. I didn't know it would be so—I don't like the way it moves."

Ruth nodded in agreement. Although she felt better out here in the open air, she clearly recalled the sick feeling in the stuffy cabin. Uncle Joe said you became used to it after awhile. He said that after a long run, sometimes he had that sick feeling when he got back on land! Uncle Joe had laughed at how many questions Ruth asked about the journey. How odd that Mrs. Graves hadn't asked hardly any at all!

Mrs. Graves finished her tea. She handed the mug to Ruth, and leaned her head back against the wagon box. Her face was still white and strained, but closer in color to what it should be.

"Thank you, dear. Would you please bring my Lucy to me? She doesn't much like this boat either."

"Certainly, ma'am," Ruth replied, but it was her private opinion that the girl would grow to like it sooner if

20

she weren't forced to attend a nervous mother. Loring and Henry, Mrs. Graves' sons, were already climbing in the rigging, trying to keep up with the sailors.

Ruth did as she was bid, however, and as she made her way to rejoin Mariah, she was hailed by one of the men in a large, noisy group.

"You! Girl!" Someone called in loud voice. A man with short, gingery whiskers sticking out in all directions from his face broke away from the group and took her by the elbow a few feet away from his friends. She drew back at the stale smell of whiskey and tobacco. Ruth remembered that smell from when Daidí took her to the horse fair at the tavern in the lower village. The man was Mr. Graves.

"How's she doing?" he asked, jerking his head toward his wife huddled on the deck.

"She's feeling a little better, sir. She's sick from the rocking of the ship. I brought her some tea."

"That's a good girl," he said approvingly. "That gal of mine should be caring for her stepmother, but those two just don't get on. Well, the missus will get over her sickness soon enough, I expect. I know I had some rough times on my last trip." He laughed uproariously at the memory.

"Perhaps if you went to her, sir," Ruth ventured, but he had already released her elbow and turned toward his companions, eager to share his seasick story as loudly and humorously as possible.

21

Ruth was hailed again before she reached the group of girls. This time it was her mother. She was sitting with the aunts on the trap door of the hold, all of them knitting and chatting as fast as they could. The little Naper cousins were bedded down in the cabin with Gran, so Aunt Betsy and Aunt Almeda had a few moments to talk over matters not fit for youngsters. Whether Mrs. Sisson's interesting condition would hold off until she made it to Fort Dearborn was the current topic. Ruth only heard a snippet about how "a ship is no birthing room" before a glance from Mother caught her attention.

"How is Mrs. Graves?" Mother asked in a low voice without looking up.

"Tolerable. She doesn't like the way the ship moves." Having answered the question, Ruth waited silently as a child should, seen but not heard. "But I'm nearly not a child," she thought, "I might be married in a few years just like Sally Ann." Ruth simply had to speak her mind. Taking a deep breath, the words escaped in a rush: "Mrs. Graves is afraid, and she doesn't know anything about ships, and Mr. Graves should have told her, but now he won't go to her, and her stepdaughter Louisa is just plain rude."

Mother raised her head to look fully into Ruth's face, her eyes full of surprise at this rare outburst from her normally unflappable child. Mother's lips pressed into a tight line, and Ruth feared she had been too forward. But then she saw the tightness twitch a little as Mother tried

22

to banish a smile.

"A wise woman would ask questions before a journey like this." Mother said, her eyebrows arching as she added in a dry voice, "And a wise man would tell her even when she didn't ask! You show more wisdom than either of those two have managed. Still, it's a shame for that poor woman to suffer so. I'll go speak to her."

Ruth didn't even realize she had been standing so stiffly, but she relaxed now, and so did Mother's mouth. She let the smile out and gave Ruth's cheek a quick caress.

"I've been so busy with Sally Ann's new baby and this move to Illinois I didn't notice how much you've been growing up these past months. Run along now to your new friends for a while. I'll need your help by and by, but I'll come for you then."

Relieved to back away from her foray into adult concerns, Ruth hurried over to the circle of girls. They were playing a handclap game again, so Ruth waited for her turn, her thoughts in a muddle. So many different sorts of people! How strange that they chose to come together to be members of this new community.

The chance to buy cheap land was a powerful pull for men on small farms in the eastern states. Uncle Joe and Uncle Jack were leaving more and more settlers behind on their western runs along the Great Lakes shore. Mr. Graves himself had toured the new state of Illinois. Men on their way west often stayed at his tavern in

Ashtabula, and a couple of travelers talked him into coming along. Leaving Mrs. Graves to manage the tavern alone, he took several long scouting trips to Illinois, and when he came home from the last one, he had his wife start packing.

For many nights Ruth lay half-awake in the loft with the other children, listening to her parents as they discussed whether to move west. Uncle Joe had a plan. He had thought it through, and he figured a new community could be successfully settled in a short time if a group of neighbors went together and supported each other.

Daidí and Mother remembered well how hard it was to settle a new land. They had been among the first who snuggled down between the wide lake and the forested cliffs of Ohio. Uncle Joe and Uncle Jack had been little boys then, living with Gran and Grandfather. But Ashtabula was a real town now with a school, neighbors, and ships in the harbor bringing goods from New York and the world. Ruth's mother and father were reluctant to leave all of that.

But Ruth knew Daidí worried. His farm was small, not enough for both his sons to live on and raise families. Mr. Babbit, their neighbor and Sally Ann's new father-in-law, had the same fears for Henry and his younger boys. Everyone heard land was plentiful farther west, and Uncle Joe promised, if they all went together, if they all did their part—

24

Mariah was inviting her into the circle for the next game, and Ruth shrugged off her jumbled thoughts. While she didn't exactly know what her part in Uncle Joe's plan was yet, she reckoned it wasn't a very important one. Grown-up concerns could wait a little longer.

Ruth By Lake And Prairie

CHAPTER 3

A GLIMPSE OF CLEVELAND

The wind continued to pick up all afternoon, driving the women and small children into the cabin. Unpredictable gusts required all the sailors' skills to keep the *Telegraph* headed in the right direction. Still, Uncle Jack expected to make Cleveland before evening.

The children were given supper early so it wouldn't be forgotten in the bustle of dropping anchor and unloading. Uncle Jack and Uncle Joe expected to trade some barrels of coffee for corn to take to the new settlement. Many passengers undoubtedly would wish to go ashore to see what they could of the city before darkness fell. Never having seen a big city before, Ruth hoped she would be allowed to go ashore as well.

The sun was low on the horizon when Cleveland was sighted. Unlike Ashtabula, there were no green cliffs backing the city, just a broad, flat plain with rolling hills and timber far behind. The city was flat and sprawling as well, spiked here and there by fancy church steeples. Raw, newly built frame houses mixed with old weathered log cabins. Several neighborhoods boasted tall, prettily painted homes belonging to those whose fortunes had

27

grown along with the city. Mariah squeezed in among the crowd watching from the rail, pulling Ruth along with her.

Log Cabin
A house built with whole or squared-off logs stacked on top of each other and notched in the corners to hold together.

"My goodness!" Ruth gasped. "I've never seen so many buildings all in one place!"

"Buffalo is just like this," Mariah assured her. "Well, maybe not quite as big yet. But definitely more elegant. They have lots of brick houses and hardly any log cabins at all."

"That's because they all burned down. My Daidí told me that Buffalo was set on fire during the 1812 war. Nearly everything burned to the ground."

"How awful!" Mariah exclaimed. "You never could tell now. You should see all the houses and churches and schools. They even have a library."

Ruth felt a tugging at her skirt and looked around. It was Amos, reaching between two women to get her attention.

"Mother says come right now!" he said, giving one last tug before disappearing behind the knot of women. Ruth promised Mariah she'd be back soon, and made her way to the other side of the ship.

Uncle Joe stood surrounded by the aunts and cousins, giving orders as if he were directing an invasion. Although daylight was fading, he declared it a shame to miss seeing such a grand city. And as was his habit, Uncle Joe had a plan to make the most of this opportunity.

"We'll want to be first off the ship since we won't have much time. Everyone grab a child's hand and follow me. Stay together! Ned, you'd better escort your Gran. We can't have you getting knocked off the pier, now can we, Ma?" Leaving Uncle Jack and his crew to unload, Uncle Joe led them past the long sheds along the wharf and down the wide streets.

Ruth gripped Amos tightly with one hand and Cordelia with the other, but both were so overwhelmed they wouldn't have strayed anyhow. Throngs of people eddied around their group, hurrying to finish their business before nightfall. The children found

Frame House
A house built with a "skeleton" covered over with a "skin" of clapboard.

themselves out of breath trying to keep up with Uncle Joe. While he mainly sailed the eastern run to Buffalo, he had stopped in Cleveland when scouting west for the new settlement, and he was eager to show off its wonders to his wife and family.

Uncle Joe found an out of the way patch of lawn on the town square where he gathered his panting followers. "This is the courthouse," he announced, gesturing toward an impressive building fully three stories tall. "It's only two years old. Why, in a few years, we could have a grand courthouse just like this in our new town!"

"Could we really, Uncle Joe?" Ruth asked, suspiciously. Even Ashtabula didn't have a three-story courthouse yet. How would Uncle Joe manage to build one in the wilderness?

Mother answered for him. "We could, but more likely we'll have nice, snug farmhouses with plenty of food in the larder. And that would be grand enough for me!"

While the courthouse reigned as the largest building on the square, the buildings surrounding it were also imposing. Uncle Joe pointed out a church with a tall spire built entirely of stone! Ruth wondered how it would sound to sing hymns in a soaring space like that, so different from the one-room log school they sang in back home.

Her strength failing her, Granny Naper asked to return to the ship. Uncle Joe led his little band through the maze of twilight-shadowed streets back to the pier. It was quite dark by the time they arrived. The clouds hid what little moon was rising.

Sailors had thrown open the door of the hold to haul out the coffee barrels and make room for the corn. Mother led Gran and the children straight to the cabin, pretending she didn't hear the shouts and oaths of the men. Amos grinned from ear to ear, but Cordelia was outraged.

"Mama! Did you hear what that man said? He said—"

"I heard him, Cordelia. You needn't repeat it," Mother replied firmly.

They entered the small cabin where some of the passengers were already preparing sleeping arrangements. Almost thirty men, women, and children had boarded the ship in Ashtabula earlier in the day. To Ruth's eye, about the same number of people were already onboard from Buffalo and Dunkirk. Space in the cabin would be tight tonight.

Two women shoved the table against one wall, bedding children down both beneath it and atop it. The curtain that could divide the room into men's quarters and women's quarters was left pulled aside. With so many women and children, the men would have to sleep elsewhere.

When Gran saw the hammocks strung from the ceiling, she folded her arms stubbornly across her chest. "I am certainly not climbing into one of those!"

"Of course not, Gran," Aunt Almeda soothed. "I've been sleeping on this bench since Dunkirk just so I could reserve it for your use. I'll bed down over here with Robbie and my girls."

Mother and Aunt Betsy found a few feet of bare floor and started to lay out their quilts. Mariah had already insisted that there would be enough room for Ruth and Cordelia to squeeze in next to her and her sisters. Growing up in a one-room cabin, Ruth was used to sleeping three or four to a bed, welcoming the company during the cold of winter. On this June night the cabin felt a bit close, but Ruth was used to that, too.

Ned and the other men took their blankets out on deck. Once the loading was complete, they would sleep under the stars or try to get comfortable in the hold among the crates and barrels. Amos begged to be allowed to go with them, but Mother forbade it for fear he would fall overboard with the rolling of the ship.

As soon as they had wrapped up in their quilt and wedged themselves into a sliver of space on the cabin floor, Cordelia surprised Ruth by falling asleep almost at once. Ruth was sure she herself would never be able to sleep. Outside the cabin the sailors still swore and sang as they banged cargo into the hold. The rigging creaked and waves slapped against the sides of the ship. Inside it was uncomfortably stuffy and smelled of tar, mildew, and sweat. Some of the women were already snoring gustily, while Mariah whispered non-stop in Ruth's ear about how delighted she was with Cleveland.

The sounds and smells were so different from back home. Caught up in the excitement of her first trip away from Ashtabula, Ruth hadn't realized before how much she would miss the quiet farm she had left behind. Daidi would right now be sitting near the fireplace, maybe just finishing his solitary supper. The empty cabin must look forlorn since all of their belongings were sold or packed on the *Telegraph*. In a few days, Daidí would leave, too, driving the cattle overland to meet the ship at Fort Dearborn. Now he was just minding the farm until the new owners took possession.

Perhaps, Ruth thought, he was singing as he often did when the flames died down and the room glowed coal-red and shadowy. Daidí liked to sing the old Irish ballads that his mother had sung to him when he was young, as well as the hymns and patriotic songs he used to teach when he was Ashtabula's first schoolmaster. Nearly every night of her life, Ruth fell asleep in the loft listening to Daidí sing, but tonight she was too far away to hear him.

Tears seeped into the shawl she was using as a pillow. With her heart and head so full, Ruth wondered how she could politely tell Mariah to stop whispering, but before she could frame the sentence, she was as fast asleep as Cordelia.

Singing woke her in the morning, although not Daidí's. It was barely light, but apparently Uncle Jack could see well enough to maneuver the ship safely out of the harbor because he was shouting orders to his crew. They started singing a shanty, one voice calling a line and the others responding in a peculiar, grunting rhythm. Mariah bolted upright.

"They're weighing anchor! We must be leaving Cleveland. Come on—let's go up and see!"

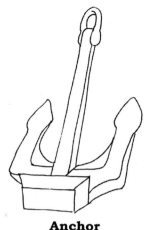

Anchor
A heavy object attached by a rope to a ship. Thrown overboard, it keeps the ship in one place.

Awed by her brief glimpse the night before, Ruth was eager to see the city one last time. So much bigger than Ashtabula! Daidí would hardly believe it when she told him. Ruth peeled back her share of the quilt and laid it over Cordelia, who was still sleeping. A few of the other women were creeping up the steps as well.

It was another cloudy, windy morning, feeling especially cool after a night spent with Cordelia snuggled against her. In the gray light, Cleveland spread out like a map with its straight roads, square gardens, and white picket fences. Ruth could almost trace the route Uncle Joe had taken them last night: the wharf, the town square, and the towering courthouse.

Mariah sighed with rapture. "Such an elegant city! If only we could settle here! I'm sure they hold dances in those big hotels. We would go together and have so many partners and eat little cakes and—"

"But we're farmer's daughters!" Ruth interrupted. "I'm sure I don't know what my Daidí would do with himself in a fancy city like this, all full of people. If he can see a neighbor's fence post from the cabin door he thinks it's too crowded!"

"My Pa says the same thing. Still, we might hold some dances, don't you think? Maybe at a barn-raising? Maybe in a town not too far away?" Mariah's voice trailed off as Cleveland disappeared behind them in the early morning mist. Shops, roads, hotels—these would all be far in the future for the new settlement. Just securing the basics of a home and food supply would take all their energies. The girls watched until the last church spire was out of sight. Then they returned to the cabin to help ready it for breakfast.

Ruth By Lake And Prairie

CHAPTER 4

THE LONG, WAKEFUL NIGHT

The gray sunrise never warmed beyond that pale, cold light. The previous day's stiff breeze continued to pick up and capped the deepening waves with white froth. When young Ira Carpenter lost his hat overboard in an unexpected gust, the men took to leaving their hats in the cabin or wrapping them to their heads with scarves as if it were winter.

Mother waved Ruth over from where the children huddled together. The wind snatched her words away as soon as they were spoken, so Mother had to raise her voice to be heard.

"I'm going into the cabin with Sally Ann for a while. This wind is something cruel to a woman's complexion! I'm sure I'm quite red by now."

"Not at all!" Ruth protested loyally, but even she was beginning to feel battered by the constant gale. When Ruth went in later for a welcome hot dinner of beans, she was reluctant to go back out. The little ones, however, could not be convinced to sit quietly inside. At a look from Mother, Ruth and Mariah gathered up the restless children and led them out for a brisk walk around the deck.

"I know!" Mariah exclaimed, bending down to the children's level to be heard above the wind. "Let's pretend that we are all French Canadian fur traders—caught in a blizzard!"

"I don't want to be French. I'm an Ojibwa brave!" Amos interrupted, letting out an ear-splitting war whoop.

"All right, you can be our Indian guide. Now, here's the story: Our canoes have been dashed to pieces on the icy rocks and we have to find our way back to the trading post in this horrid blizzard. O brave Indian guide, lead the way!"

Mariah grasped the back of Amos's trousers and took her sister Harriet's hand. Harriet grabbed Addie, and they all lined up, with Ruth bringing up the rear. Each child held on to the one in front and in back so they wouldn't be blown off course by the pretend blinding snow, which was not far from the truth of the situation.

A few turns around the deck were not nearly enough to tire the enthusiastic "fur traders," but a sudden downpour interrupted their exercise and sent them all scurrying inside.

As she stood in the doorway Ruth couldn't believe they would all fit into the tiny cabin, but somehow even she was able to get in out of the rain. The wall-to-wall humanity wriggled like a handful of fishing worms, and the stale air was not improved by the smell of wet woolen jackets. At least Ruth was able to wedge herself in near

Mariah so they could talk. Since they were last in, they found a sliver of space near the door, which didn't fit very tightly in its frame. They were frequently sprayed with rain driven in by the wind, but they also had the advantage of an occasional fresh breeze.

At first, the sudden gale was rather fun. The children chattered excitedly about their escape from the deluge that pounded on the cabin roof. In a short while, the din increased. Deep rolling thunder grew nearer and louder until swift stabs of lightning proved the storm to be directly on them.

Mariah clutched at Ruth in dramatic bliss. "Oh my! That one was close! Have you ever seen anything so thrilling?"

Ruth shook her head doubtfully. "The others don't seem to think it's thrilling. Next time the lightning flashes, take a look at your mother's face. She looks worried. So does my mother."

The thundering ebbed and flowed as individual squalls passed over them, but the rain never ceased drumming on the roof and deck, and the wind howled above it all. Eventually, the children caught their elders' apprehension and quieted.

Outside, Ruth could hear Uncle Jack and Uncle Joe shouting to the crew, who rushed about preparing the *Telegraph* to ride out the storm. With no safe harbor near, Uncle Jack fought his way farther out on the lake for fear they would be driven up on rocks along the coast.

Sails were reduced and secured. Rigging, loose against the masts, was tied down. Uncle Jack ordered the sailors to "Let out the ropes!" Long and heavy, the ropes dragged behind the ship to keep her facing into the wind, breaking the waves. If the little schooner were hit from the side, she could easily roll over. Even with all the crew's skill, the *Telegraph* rocked and bobbed like a twig in a millstream.

Caught up in the urgency of the storm and refreshed by the draft from the door, Ruth didn't notice the rolling of the ship at first. But just when she could no longer ignore the uncomfortable feeling in her stomach, someone in the back of the cabin was sick into the chamber pot.

As uncomfortable as the passengers thought they already were, it soon became much worse. In the humid, stinking cabin, several people were sick in succession. It became essential to empty the pot. Mariah's mother held it out for her daughter to take, but Mariah shrank away with both hands over her mouth, shaking her head violently.

"I'll do it," Ruth said between gritted teeth. "Even getting drenched has to be better than staying in here." She shrugged off her shawl and bonnet, figuring she might as well have some dry clothes to return to. Then Ruth picked up the chamber pot.

Once Ruth unlatched the door, wind snatched it from her fingers and slammed it against the outer wall of the cabin. Cold rain slanted into the room. As quickly as possible, Ruth moved outside and closed the door behind her. Already soaked through, Ruth turned her back to the wind and moved toward the corner of the cabin. She slid one bare foot after the other along the flooded deck, hindered by the long skirt plastered against her legs.

As she rounded the corner, where there was no more protection from the cabin wall, a strong gust shoved her along the slippery boards. Unable to regain her footing, Ruth flailed wildly with one arm, the other still wrapped around the reeking pot. The driving rain blinded her so she couldn't see where to grab, and she knew in a moment both she and the chamber pot would be over the rail.

Someone seized her skirt from behind, yanking her hard onto her backside. Her legs splayed out in front of her awkwardly, but her dress no longer was a sail in the wind. Sheltering her face with her free arm, she looked up to see Uncle Joe with a face nearly as stormy as the sky.

"What the devil are you doing on deck? You could have been washed overboard!" He shouted over the wind.

Uncle Joe pulled her up against the platform where Uncle Jack fought with the ship's wheel. Both men wore leather cape-like coats that protected them somewhat from the elements and brimmed hats wrapped tightly to their heads to keep the rain out of their eyes.

"What the devil are you doing out on deck?" Uncle Joe

repeated.

"Everyone is sick inside. Someone had to empty this—" Ruth glanced down at the pot in her lap, rapidly filling with water and threatening to overflow on her skirt.

Joe threw a comment over his shoulder to Jack that Ruth couldn't hear, and both men laughed uproariously. Uncle Joe took the pot from her and tossed its contents in the direction of the back of the ship. Within seconds, the rain and waves rinsed the deck clean.

The uncles held a few minutes of shouted conversation. Then Uncle Joe squatted down beside her and spoke directly in her ear.

"I'll take you back to the cabin, but there will be no more pleasure strolls until this storm passes, do you understand?" Cold and battered, Ruth eagerly agreed. Risking a glance up at him, she was surprised to see Uncle Joe was not nearly as angry as he sounded.

He hauled her to her feet and threw part of his cape over her. "You're a strong-hearted girl, Ruth Eliza, and a willing one. But it's not your place to be out here right now."

Uncle Joe pulled his hat a little lower over his eyes and took the chamber pot from her. "Well, let's go. Keep your head down and hang on to my coattail."

As they fought their way along the cabin wall, Uncle Joe's eyes searched the far horizon. "I don't see a break in the clouds yet," he muttered under his breath. "In fact, it looks darker out west and there's no bay to shelter in nearby. The best we can do is to keep her pointed into the storm so we aren't broadsided."

He stopped speaking suddenly and chuckled. "But don't you go telling those people in the cabin any of this! They're spooked enough already!"

When they made it to the door, Uncle Joe thrust Ruth in and ordered the miserable crowd not to leave the cabin until he said so. Then he slammed the door shut and left them.

No one spoke, although Ruth could see everyone's eyes were on her as she stood where Uncle Joe had left her with the rain puddling around her feet. Mother's face twisted, threatening to weep with remorse and relief, but Ruth managed a weak smile behind her wet, straggling hair. She held out her hands.

"I brought back the pot."

For a moment there was stunned silence, then Gran snickered from the farthest corner, which started Aunt Betsy giggling, and before long the entire room echoed with nervous laughter. The tension eased, and people started talking loudly, as if determined to drown out the noise of the storm.

Happy to no longer be the center of attention, Ruth sank to the floor in an exhausted heap. Mariah gave her back her bonnet and shawl, but Ruth was too tired to put them on. They sat side by side quietly as Ruth's racing heart slowed to normal.

"You were so brave! To go out into such a terrible

storm!" Mariah cast a sideways glance at Ruth. "If I hadn't been so ill, I would have gone. It must have been a terribly thrilling adventure!"

"No, it wasn't." Ruth replied in a flat voice. Mariah raised her eyebrows in disbelief, but she held her tongue, sensing Ruth was in no mood for fine tales.

Although they hadn't seen the sun all day, the darkness deepened as suppertime approached. The ship was tossing too much to cook on the stove, but Mary passed mugs of cool water around with the hard biscuits for those who felt able to eat something. The retching had continued all afternoon and into the evening, and few folks were able to keep their dinner down.

The furious lightning storms passed, subsiding into a heavy rain that fell steadily as night advanced. With no moon or stars Ruth couldn't see even Mariah lying next to her, but she could feel the people pressed in all around. They were breathing lightly, quietly, as if they were all asleep, but Ruth could tell they were wakeful. During brief lulls in the wind, a constant weary weeping could be heard from Mrs. Graves.

Ruth jerked awake at the sound of flapping canvas. Uncle Jack must have ordered the sails hoisted. Rain continued to beat on the roof, but the wind did sound less fitful. Slight differences in the shadows told Ruth that dawn must be breaking.

Others stirred in the darkness and Ruth heard whispering. A baby woke up fussing, but the cries turned to noisy suckling as the mother fed it. On the other side of the door from Ruth, young Mrs. Strong was getting to her feet. A bride of just a couple months, she had burst into tears when her husband left the cabin the night before with the other gentlemen. With the cabin so crowded, the men went below to make their beds atop the cargo. While sleeping on top of barrels and crates was uncomfortable enough normally, Ruth suspected that the rain leaking in had made it even worse.

Trying to be quiet, Mrs. Strong pulled back the latch on the door. Her slim shadow passed through the pale gray rectangle of light outlined by the doorway. A fresh breeze rushed in, rousing the sleepers more than the noise of the latch.

Ruth nudged Mariah. "Let's get out."

"It's still raining," Mariah whispered back. After fighting nausea all night, Mariah looked like she just wanted to stay curled up on the floor with her eyes screwed shut.

"You'll feel better outside. Honestly!"

Ruth helped Mariah up and they slipped out the door. Ruth felt wobbly in the knees, but a few deep breaths of cool air calmed her churning belly. By standing on the starboard side of the cabin they gained a little protection from the rain. Their only view on this side, however, was where the lake met the sky. Both were so colorless Ruth couldn't even tell where the horizon was.

Poking her head around the corner, Ruth saw that

they were much farther from land than the day before. An unbroken line of trees along the shore stretched smoothly both ahead and behind with nothing resembling a cove or harbor.

One by one, green-faced women and children emerged from the reeking cabin, gulping in great lungsful of fresh air, turning their faces to the rain. The men came up from the hold looking equally ill and rather sodden.

"Listen," Ruth said.

Mariah cocked her head. "That's Mary, lighting the stove."

"Yes, I know. To make breakfast. But look at us! Who's going to eat it?" Ruth gestured toward the other passengers, who all looked damp, sick, and miserable.

Mariah managed a weak giggle. "You're right! It would just be a waste of food!"

Once the sun was fully up, Uncle Jack left the wheel to his first mate, Mr. Smith, and climbed wearily down from his platform. Together with Uncle Joe, he retired to the cabin for a hot meal. Most of the men followed to hear the news, even if they couldn't bring themselves to eat. Mr. Strong, hatless and with his black hair curling from the damp, stayed outside with an arm around his young wife. The rest of the passengers huddled on the deck, as oblivious to the rain as cattle in the field.

"It seems a little lighter out that way," someone ventured.

"But the weather's coming from the west. It's not

lighter out west."

"Why doesn't Captain Naper put in somewhere until it passes?"

One of the women spoke up decisively. "Can't," Mrs. Boardman said. "No harbor from here until Port Lawrence. And that's chancy in rough water. Rocks."

Uneasy silence rested on them until one of the ladies from Buffalo said, "It's not quite like New York, is it?"

"No, it's the frontier," Aunt Betsy chuckled. "Is this the adventure our husbands promised us?"

"I think even they have had enough adventure this morning!" Aunt Almeda retorted, and everyone laughed, but their worried eyes still searched the dark western skies.

CHAPTER 5

ANOTHER DAY, ANOTHER NIGHT

Even before the children finished breakfast, the waves started to swell. Passengers crowded into the cabin as the temperature dropped and the rain increased. Uncle Jack and half of his men had retired, exhausted, to the crew's quarters to snatch a few hours rest, leaving Uncle Joe at the wheel. He was also red-eyed and weary, but judged it best to let the *Telegraph*'s captain sleep. Mrs. Boardman's husband, also a Great Lakes captain, went up to offer his help.

In the cabin, folks complained and quarreled. After facing last night's storm, bravado made light of this new threat. Without fear to quiet them, the children were restless and bored. Mothers scolded and boxed ears, but since the children couldn't be sent away, the noise just increased and nerves were rubbed raw.

Eventually the youngsters were sent into one small corner to wrestle and poke each other, and Ruth found herself next to Mrs. Graves. Although no one had slept much the previous night, Mrs. Graves had continued to weep in unrelenting despair even when the others managed to doze. No longer crying, Mrs. Graves simply stared straight ahead now. In her lap, her hands twisted in constant motion. They were red and chapped, but she didn't seem aware of them at all.

"Mrs. Graves?" Ruth ventured. "Mrs. Graves?"

The woman showed no sign that she heard. Ruth watched her for a long moment, then slowly reached out and took both of Mrs. Graves' hands in her own. They fluttered at first, but soon calmed in Ruth's firm grasp. Ruth marveled at how slim and elegant Mrs. Graves' fingers were. Her own hands were large and pale, with torn nails and calluses from rough work. Mother was always after Ruth to trim her nails and rub her hands with lard to soften the skin, but Ruth never bothered. Ruth's hands certainly weren't very ladylike, but they were strong and warm and steady as she held those of Mrs. Graves'.

In the swirl of noise from the children, the rain, and the flapping sails, Ruth sat patiently. Her thoughts wandered back to Ashtabula, and she realized it was Sunday. At home they might just be leaving the schoolhouse where the villagers gathered for Sunday Meeting. Sometimes a traveling preacher would be on hand to lead the service and preach loud and long enough to last until his next circuit. More often the schoolteacher or another gentleman would read from the Bible and Daidí would lead the singing of the hymns.

The first settlers of Ashtabula had built a school almost immediately, and Ruth loved to hear the story of how Daidí took up the job of schoolmaster while he cleared the land for his own farm. He boarded with the settlers and taught their children to read and write and sing. Daidí liked to say it was his fine voice at Sunday Meeting that Mother fell in love with during the time she kept house for her brother Ben.

Smiling to herself, Ruth wondered which hymns Daidí had led that morning. Maybe "The Spirit Shall Return" or "O Holy Manna"? One of Ruth's favorites, in Daidí's lowest, most melancholy tones, was "Wayfaring Stranger." She hummed the first line to herself.

I am a poor wayfaring stranger
Traveling through this world of woe...

"How odd!" she thought. "Very like us now!" She continued humming to see if she could catch other similarities.

Yet there's no sickness, no toil or danger
In that bright world to which I go.

Concentrating on the words, Ruth barely realized that Mrs. Graves was singing along in a choked voice. As if she gained strength from the song, the woman's voice swelled with every line. On the other side of her, Mrs. Wilson picked up the tune.

I know dark clouds will gather around me.
I know my way is rough and steep.
Yet beauteous fields lie just before me
Where God's redeemed their vigils keep.

Before long the entire room was singing. Strained faces relaxed. The children stopped fidgeting. When they came to the next refrain, the families from Ashtabula broke into the harmonies Daidí had taught them, Sally Ann's high, pure soprano dancing over the rest. They sang with such feeling that the sounds of the storm outside were drowned out.

Mariah and the other girls from New York watched Sally Ann sing with something like hero-worship. Ruth was not surprised. Sally Ann drew admirers in Ashtabula, too. She was Daidí's star pupil, with an enchantingly lyrical voice that matched her blooming beauty. Secretly, Ruth liked to hear Sally Ann sing as much as anyone, but whenever people started gushing about how talented her older sister was, Ruth couldn't help but be annoyed.

Ruth let her eyes wander around the room. Everyone was singing, and most of them were looking at Sally Ann. Except Mother, who was looking right back at Ruth. Mother's eyes sparkled proudly like they always did when she watched Sally Ann sing. But this time she wasn't watching Sally Ann, and Ruth felt the warmth of Mother's approval all the way across the room.

Hymn-singing carried them through most of the afternoon. Toward evening the rain eased up enough for passengers to go out on deck and stretch their legs, so the stove was quickly lit to heat water for tea. Not knowing how long the lull might last, the women chose to break off some chunks of portable soup for supper. Dissolved in water, the broth would serve as a hot meal for the exhausted sailors.

After his brief nap, Uncle Jack returned to the wheel, determined to make Port Lawrence before nightfall. But even using the combined skills of the crew and the other two lake captains on board, the *Telegraph* hardly made headway. The sun slipped beneath the horizon, the pale western light faded, and still there was no sign of Maumeee Bay.

Portable Soup
Dried broth, like a bouillon cube, that would not spoil during a long trip and could be reconstituted with water when needed.

A new surge of driving rain sent people scurrying inside again. On deck everyone kept busy scouring the shoreline for signs of civilization, and mentally urging the little ship forward. Now, with nothing to see through the small, steamed up windows, they could only hope and pray.

Thunder rumbled, low and ominous, in the distance. Conversation dwindled to often-repeated variations of "Shouldn't we be there by now?" Then the wind picked up, flapping the sails furiously and heralding the squall bearing down on them.

A sailor shouted outside, but his words were carried away when suddenly the storm broke over them. A great clap of thunder rattled the windows of the cabin, the lightning bolt so bright for a moment Ruth thought it had struck them. The drumming of rain on the roof was deafening. Although Ruth could see the children's mouths wide open at every flash, she could not hear their cries.

As the storm went on and on, Ruth began to feel as if in a dream. The constant assault of noise and light and motion numbed her. Surely there was no other world beyond this small, humid room filled with faces that didn't move, but were glimpsed in jerky flashes, as if she were flipping through a book of drawings. Only occasionally did shouting voices in a momentary lull prove the crew was still doggedly at their duties.

Time passed. Minutes or hours, Ruth could not tell. Fear paralyzed everyone at the beginning, but then their bellies could no longer ignore the violent rolling and pitching of the little ship. Water began seeping through the door and around the windows, adding to the misery of anyone seated nearby. The smells of sickness and wet wool were overwhelming, and when Mariah beside her was sick into the pot, Ruth couldn't help but join her.

In later years, whenever the preacher talked about hell, Ruth thought of that night. At the time, however,

Ruth wasn't thinking at all. Like dumb animals, she and the others simply endured, hour after hour.

It was with surprise that Ruth noticed, between lightning strikes, that the darkness was fading. Morning had arrived without the ship ever landing at Port Lawrence.

Although clouds hid the sun, Ruth figured it was midmorning by the time the rumbling of thunder faded and no new squall swept across their bow. Rough waves still battered the little ship and a penetrating rain refused to let up, but the relative quiet was a relief. People began to stir, hopeful that the calm would continue, when the door suddenly burst open.

Captain Jack Naper stood in the doorway, water streaming from his clothes. His broad shoulders sagged and his face was weary, but his eyes betrayed nothing dreadful. Aunt Betsy struggled to her feet and tried to go to him, but she was hemmed in on all sides.

"Oh, Jack!" she cried out, relieved.

He smiled back. "Can a body get something to eat in here?" he asked wryly.

All too eager to be doing something, women with any strength left rose as a body to shoo the children out into the rain and try to set the cabin to rights. Grateful to escape, Ruth led Cordelia, Amos, and their young cousins outside. Mariah followed with the youngsters of her family. Queasy and exhausted, they huddled together as much out of the rain as possible, breathing deeply.

As she started to feel stronger, Ruth became more aware of her surroundings. The deck was littered with debris apparently blown in during the storm. Ropes, normally neatly coiled, snaked among the wagon boxes and other cargo. The cargo itself, fortunately, remained secured, but had shifted and would need retying. The flag was shredded and the sails looked a little tattered as well, but the most glaring damage was raw splintered wood where the mainmast boom had cracked in two.

Mr. Smith was at the wheel. All of the other adults were jammed into the tiny cabin, spilling out of the doorway. Ned and some of the boys had clambered onto the roof of the cabin, hanging over to peer in the doorway. Something was happening inside.

Boom

The long pole at right angles to the mast that holds the bottom of the sail taut.

Ruth nudged Mariah and pointed. Voices rose and fell from within, but they couldn't make out the words.

"Ned!" Ruth hissed. "What's going on?"

Ned shook his head. His face scrunched up as he concentrated on trying to hear the conversation. Voices swelled with anger and fear, but soon Ruth heard Uncle Joe calmly speaking until everyone else grew quiet again. After a while some of the passengers drifted out on deck and meal preparation began.

The boys slipped off the cabin roof and went over to where Ruth and Mariah waited with the children. "Well?" Mariah demanded.

Ned was examining the broken boom, so Mariah's half-brother Allen answered. "We missed the Maumee River Bay during the storm. Captain Naper didn't want to get too near for fear of the rocks, but then we were blown north and missed it altogether. In fact, we're so far north now that he's headed straight for Detroit. With this wind and missing a sail, we couldn't possibly get back to Port Lawrence."

"How far away is Detroit?"

"They reckon another day or so. There were no stars last night to take a reading, and we're too far away to look for landmarks." Allen paused for a moment, his eye on the horizon.

Following his gaze, the girls realized for the first time that they were no longer tracing the outline of the shore. Only gray water met gray sky in every direction they looked. The little ship, battered and crippled, drifted alone on the cold, choppy lake.

Ned returned from studying the boom, shaking his head. "Well, I don't know much about it, but I don't see that we'll make very good time with just one sail. Especially if it storms again." He looked up and met Ruth's eyes. "Let's pray it doesn't storm."

RUTH BY LAKE AND PRAIRIE

CHAPTER 6

AN ARRIVAL AND A DEPARTURE

I t rained more. It rained less. Ruth remembered little else of that long, long day. No lightning or thunder threatened them. No sunshine ever reached out for them through the heavy cloud cover. Rough waters kept the ship pitching and rolling, and drove the nauseous passengers on deck for fresh air. There they sat silently until the rain chilled them through. Some were quite ill and weak from not having kept a meal down for days.

When night fell they were still out of sight of land. Too cold to stay out in the wet, Ruth and the others tried to settle into the cabin or below deck. The lucky ones fell into a fitful sleep. Ruth dozed, but frequently woke to cries of the children or moans of the sick. Every time she opened her eyes, she prayed to see daylight.

A shout out on deck startled her awake. Visible forms in the darkness of the cabin proved that the night was finally ending. The shout outside was repeated: "Land! Starboard side!"

The dark forms struggled to their feet and pushed their way out the door. Ruth followed with Cordelia in tow. Jostled by the eager crowd, Ruth strained on tiptoe to see. Shrouded in mist and barely visible in the predawn light, the horizon looked as blank and gray as before. Then a line of shadow in the distance shimmered and became more distinct. It was land!

Time still moved nightmarishly slowly, but the *Telegraph* drew nearer and nearer to the shoreline. Eventually, they entered the wide mouth of a river. Here and there were cabins and fields with seedling crops in the clearings among the forest. Occasionally even people could be seen as they went about their chores. Although they were too far away to halloo at, sometimes they waved as the ship passed.

Ruth heard muttering among the passengers who wanted to put in immediately. Mrs. Sisson, who had endured the storm with hardly a murmur, now appeared quite ill and her husband was the most vocal about going ashore. Uncle Jack finally called the passengers out on deck to speak to them. Ruth gathered with her aunts and cousins near the ship's wheel while Uncle Jack explained that Detroit offered the best place to have the *Telegraph* repaired so to Detroit they would continue.

Aunt Betsy glanced at the Sissons and tugged at Uncle Jack's sleeve. "How long until we reach Detroit?" she whispered.

"If the weather doesn't change again, we should be able to tie up in a few hours."

Once more Aunt Betsy looked to Mrs. Sisson, who nodded her head. All the women exchanged meaningful glances, but Ruth was too tired to wonder. Not until Aunt Betsy asked her to keep Mariah and her sisters occupied on the foredeck did the significance strike her.

"Is Mrs. Sisson ill?" Ruth asked, remembering Sally Ann's long worrisome night when Eunice was born just a few months ago.

"She's well enough. This is her fifth lying-in, so she's no stranger to motherhood. Mrs. Sisson would rather the child be born on land, but we'll just have to see what Providence chooses!" Aunt Betsy smiled reassuringly. "Take the Sisson girls away now, Ruth Eliza, and leave it to their father to tell them the news. We needn't worry them."

The younger girls vied to be first to spot Detroit. Ruth and Mariah wondered if it would be as grand as Cleveland, but even Cleveland couldn't prepare them for the first sight of Detroit. The river, so calm after the fury of Lake Erie, stretched wide enough for dozens of boats to pass without danger of colliding. On both sides were several long piers, each with accompanying warehouses, inns, and shops. Forests of tall masts bristled along the docks from tied-up ships. And beyond all the bustle of the shipyards, straight streets and frame houses extended as far as one could see. Even all these wonders were not enough to distract the battered travelers from their misery, and great was their relief when the *Telegraph* finally limped into safe harbor.

The customs collector on the wharf recommended a

Shipyard
A harbor where ships are tied to the dock to be unloaded or repaired.

nearby hotel. Close enough to walk to, soon Ruth was helping Gran and the children into the comfortable common room while Mother spoke to the innkeeper's wife about Mrs. Sisson. By midday the weary passengers had changed out of their wettest clothes and the smell of dinner being prepared almost aroused an appetite.

The heaving in their stomachs, however, had not subsided enough to risk more than some broth and bread.

With so many families quartered at the inn, Captain Jack Naper was overwhelmed with questions when he arrived. Climbing atop a bench, he held up both hands until they quieted.

"Luck was with us to make Detroit. There's no better place to tie up, and already the *Telegraph* is under repair.

We'll remain in port tonight at least, but I figure to be under way by tomorrow afternoon." The room remained quiet, and Uncle Jack laughed. "You don't look too eager to get back on board! But a hot meal and a few hours' rest will put you to rights, I promise you. That's what I intend to do!"

He yawned hugely and clambered down from his perch. Aunt Betsy drew him aside where his dinner was waiting, and stood guard over her husband while he ate. Her usually jolly face hardened along the jaw as she warned off anyone who dared to disturb his meal.

Leaving the men to their dinner, Ruth stepped outside on the porch. Several days of rain had transformed the dirt streets into rivers of mud. Raised wooden sidewalks helped keep pedestrians out of the worst of it, but exploring was out of the question. Still, with the wharf so near, there was plenty to see from the inn's porch.

Granny Naper sat on a bench near the door basking in the watery sunshine. At her feet baby Eunice lay in a basket, well swaddled and fast asleep. "Come sit for a spell," Gran invited. "At least this floor isn't bucking like a wild colt." Ruth flopped down beside her.

"Did you see Mrs. Sisson inside?" Gran asked.

"The innkeeper's wife put her in a private room. Some of the ladies are sitting with Mrs. Sisson right now. I think Mrs. Boardman and Mrs. Butterfield."

Gran nodded. "I expect those two will take particular care of Mrs. Sisson, seeing as how they're so close to being brought to bed themselves. Birthing a baby is tricky enough without being in a strange city among strange people. I'm sure it's much on their minds."

Shooed outside by their father, Mariah and her sisters joined Ruth on the porch to watch folk passing back and forth on the dirty road. A stout woman with two squawking hens in each hand slipped and slid as she made her way through the mud. Feathers flew in a cloud around her as she tried to keep her balance by waving her arms wildly.

"Oh! She's going to go down!" One of the girls exclaimed.

"No, she's all right!"

"Wait! There she goes—no, she made it!"

"The poor chickens!"

The stout woman managed to cross the road without mishap, and as she disappeared around the corner, the girls on the porch dissolved into giggles. "And only last night," Ruth marveled, "we were so miserable!"

An entire week had passed since they left Ashtabula. Ruth wondered where Daidí and Henry were. They must have started their journey overland by now. How fast would the oxen and horses walk? Even if it rained on land as hard as it did on Lake Erie, they might make better time than the *Telegraph* because oxen didn't seem to mind rain at all. But then the horses didn't much like thunder and lightning and could cause plenty of trouble. Ruth smiled to herself remembering Abbie, a mare who was spooked by falling leaves, swaying dandelions, and a long list of other harmless objects, but Ruth's thoughts were interrupted.

From within the shadowy inn, a woman's shrill voice suddenly rose to an embarrassing level. A lower voice, a man's, pleaded and soothed desperately, but the woman wouldn't quiet. Conversation dwindled on the porch as the people there tried not to listen. Obviously the woman was one of their fellow passengers because she angrily refused to have anything to do with "that boat, Captain Jack Naper, or you! And don't you think you can make me change my mind!"

Ruth didn't recognize the voice, but in a moment Mr. Graves stormed out of the inn, his neck and face red above his collar. He glanced once at all the ladies and children sitting in the sun, pretending they hadn't heard, before stomping off down the board sidewalk. Since Mrs. Graves never spoke above a whisper, Ruth was surprised to learn the owner of that unladylike shriek.

During the men's supper, Ruth heard another piercing cry from within. Mrs. Boardman came out on the porch to tell Mariah that her mother was safely delivered of a little girl.

"Five sisters!" Mariah laughed. "Poor Allen!" Then she hurried in to meet the new baby.

Mr. Graves did not return to the inn while Ruth was in the common room. Throughout the evening different women sat with Mrs. Graves in her corner and talked to her in low voices, but apparently that one burst of furious noise was an exception. In fact, she didn't speak at all, keeping her lips tightly pressed in a stubborn line and barely looking up from the Bible on her lap no matter who was sitting with her.

Even though dramas swirled all around her, the last few days had been exhausting and Ruth found herself nodding sleepily right after supper. With many of the others, she turned in early, climbing the narrow stairs up to the women's loft with her bedroll to find a space on the wooden floor for herself and Cordelia. Like the *Telegraph*'s cabin, the room was crowded and hot, but at least it didn't rock to and fro. Ruth fell soundly asleep as soon as she pulled up the quilt.

Morning dawned sunny but still cool, and the shutters of the inn were thrown open to catch the fresh breeze. Ruth woke ravenous, and grew even hungrier at the delicious smells of bacon and cornbread while the men ate. Still, the memories of seasickness were quite vivid, and she planned to eat sparingly. Uncle Joe stopped on the porch as he went out to light his pipe near the waiting children. His little Robert ran up with Amos and other youngsters to pepper him with questions about the ship's repair. He had plenty of good news, but the best news was that they would not be leaving Detroit until late afternoon, so they might eat at least one hearty meal!

Even Mother and the aunts hankered to explore after breakfast. Gran decided to watch the city from the porch, but nearly all of the other families from the *Telegraph* eagerly set off together.

Almost immediately differing tastes broke up their large party. The farmers lingered at the blacksmith and the livery stable. The children watched the newspaper press run for quite some time, but the selection of sweets at the general merchandise store lured them away. Their mothers gathered at the other end of the shop to finger bolts of printed calicos, but Mr. Peck busily poked into every nook and cranny. Intending to open a trading post of his own at the new settlement, he checked every price, noted each item's quality, and drew the shopkeeper into an intense discussion.

Finally leaving Mr. Peck to his inquiries, what was left of the group continued their tour of Detroit. Even with a June sun in a cloudless sky, the air was cool and sweet from days of rain. Spring had been late this year, wet and cold. While disappointing at the time, Ruth certainly appreciated it now on such a shining day. With no clouds of dust in the streets and no summer heat trickling sweat down her neck, Ruth was in a holiday mood.

Compared to Ashtabula, Detroit was a fairy tale city. A thriving port even when the colonies were loyal to King George, Detroit had grown bigger and richer through the generations. Little Ashtabula was settled by people like Ruth's own Mother and Daidí barely twenty-five years ago. Certainly Ashtabula boasted two-story frame houses now, but some families still lived in the original homesteaders' cabins.

No stumpy old cabins in Detroit! As far as Ruth could see, straight streets framed neat neighborhoods of beautiful tall houses with wide porches and green gardens, each one newer than the next. Later, she learned that not long before Daidí staked his claim in Ashtabula, the city of Detroit was utterly destroyed by fire. With all the shacks and cabins burnt down to the soil, the city fathers laid out a new, ambitious plan that bloomed now for the travelers from Ohio.

They marveled at the courthouse and the church spires, but too soon it was time to return to the inn. Ned met them there and guided Mother and the aunts back to the ship after dinner. Once again, Gran clutched Ruth's left arm while Cordelia hung on the right. Once again, they teetered over the gangplank from the dock. Ruth settled Gran onto her trunk in the cabin and went back up on deck to say good-bye to Detroit.

Ruth expected to find Mariah and the other passengers also on deck, enjoying the weather and the view. Instead, knots of people buzzed with excited, whispered conversations. Spying Mariah on the outskirts of a group of women, Ruth slipped in beside her.

"What's happening?" Ruth asked.

"It's the Graves family. They won't go on." Mariah pointed down the wharf to where Mr. Graves stood with Uncle Jack and Uncle Joe, both of whom looked out of patience. Finally, Uncle Jack turned to his first mate, Mr.

Smith, who stood nearby waiting, and gave his orders.

Mr. Smith bustled down the dock, shouting to the crew. Instantly, they swarmed onto the *Telegraph*, wrenching open the trap doors of the hold and starting to unload. The women onboard shook their heads as the men muttered among themselves rather loudly.

"He had all day to fetch his gear!"

"We'll be delayed for hours now!"

Mr. Graves boarded the *Telegraph*, his ginger-bearded chin stuck out defiantly, but he couldn't quite meet the eyes of the other passengers. He and Uncle Joe supervised the crew, separating the Graves family equipment from the rest. While the remaining travelers stood by to ensure the safety of their own goods, Ruth's gaze wandered around the rest of the ship. Near the ship's wheel, Ned, Allen Sisson, and both of the Graves boys were deep in serious conversation.

Ruth nudged Mariah and cocked her head in the boys' direction. "Let's see what they're up to," she whispered. The two girls slipped away from their mothers and around the cabin. Allen looked up and grimaced seeing his younger sister, but Ned motioned Ruth to join them.

"Mr. and Mrs. Graves won't go on," he explained. "Well, Mrs. Graves won't go on and Mr. Graves can't make her. But Loring and Henry here don't want to leave."

"My pa's going to buy a wagon and we're to walk to Fort Dearborn, just Ma and the girls and us. Henry and I want to stay on the *Telegraph*. It won't storm anymore, I'm sure of it! Ma will get used to it all right."

Ruth's eyebrows arched remembering Mrs. Graves' numb suffering. "Your ma will not get used to it," she said flatly. "And it's right for your pa to stay with her. You should stay, too. They'll need your help on the way. It's a long journey."

Henry sighed, and looked resigned to giving up his sailor's adventures, but Loring stuck out his chin stubbornly, the image of his father, although without the ginger whiskers.

"I won't lead a wagon to Fort Dearborn! I won't! There'll be lots of wagons when we get to the settlement, but this might be the last time I ever get to sail on a ship. Next we sail on Lake Huron, and then Lake Michigan. All they'll see from the wagon is prairie grass!"

"While we will see the great northern pine forests! And soldiers garrisoned in ancient forts!" Mariah chimed in, sensing another kindred soul. Allen snorted at such fanciful enthusiasm, but Loring turned to her in complete understanding.

"My ma says she's making this journey so I won't ever have to. So I'll have plenty of sod to break and fields to plant without ever having to go away again. But she doesn't understand! I don't want to sit on the same piece of land all my life! I want to see other places, other people—" Loring broke off with a suspicious catch in his voice.

They all examined their feet intently while Loring breathed hard for a few moments. Finally, he repeated in his normal voice: "I won't lead a wagon to Fort Dearborn."

Ruth glanced from face to face in their little circle. Nobody met her eye. They were all still embarrassed by Loring's outburst, and Ruth wondered at the strange passion that prompted it. Ned seemed perfectly content. He liked to work hard all day with his big hands and share in a friendly round of whiskey when work was done. Henry and Allen never talked of longing for more than the ordinary careers laid out for them, either. Ruth doubted if even Mariah, whose imagination sympathized with Loring's dreams, would ever really choose to break away from a conventional life.

Ruth searched Loring's face last. His jaw clenched willfully, but it was still smooth and beardless. Was he ready, she wondered, to strike out on his own and make his place in the world? Suddenly, Mr. Graves strode up to them. "Loring! Henry! Let's go!" he barked.

Henry started to follow, but Loring straightened his shoulders. "I reckon I'll stay."

"No, you won't. Come on, we've got to buy a wagon and get all this gear stowed."

"Henry can do it. You won't need me until you get to the settlement. I—I want to stay on the *Telegraph*. Please, Pa!"

Dexter Graves turned and looked fully at his oldest

son. He thought about his wife installed at the hotel. He pictured the oxen plodding through Indiana. He remembered his own travels down the Ohio and Mississippi rivers. Mr. Graves met the boy's pleading eyes and sighed. "I'll talk to Captain Naper. We'll meet you at Fort Dearborn."

Too grown up for a display of emotion, Loring barely restrained himself from throwing his arms around his father. Instead, Loring awkwardly stuck out his hand, which Mr. Graves shook in solemn ceremony. Then Mr. Graves and Henry left.

Before the flush of success faded to doubt, Ruth suggested in a mild tone that the sailors would soon be casting off. Instantly the three boys scrambled to help. Ruth and Mariah rejoined the rest of the throng amidships to take their last look at Detroit.

CHAPTER 7

THE CALM AFTER THE STORM

Sailing the Detroit River felt like a picnic excursion compared to the stormy passage of Lake Erie. Wide enough to offer plenty of safe, deep water, it was yet narrow enough to easily take in the sights of both shores. Spirits rose onboard, with nearly everyone enjoying conversation on the sunny deck.

Even Mrs. Sisson dozed comfortably in the fresh air, the new baby wrapped up with her. Mr. Sisson created a pallet for them by restacking a couple of crates and covering them with blankets, just high enough to see a bit of the scenery over the rail. Mariah stayed close to her mother, eager to be of use, so Ruth found herself drifting from group to group.

She played with her little cousins for a while, twisting her handkerchief around her fist to look like a rabbit. The rabbit puppet sang silly songs and told stories until the children lost interest and started "Ring a Ring o' Roses." Ruth tucked the handkerchief away and wandered over to where Mother and the aunts stood talking.

Mrs. Sisson's lying-in still dominated their

conversation. What the innkeeper's wife did, how Sally Ann managed when Eunice was born, and what Mrs. Butterfield and Mrs. Boardman planned when their time came endlessly looped around the circle of women. Ruth supposed one day such things would be of intense interest to her too, but that time was not now.

Although she would never dream of joining the men, she moved near enough to hear some of their discussion. The usual farming predictions and political opinions were offered, but Mr. Graves' decision to take the land route the rest of the way came in for its share.

"Never saw the woman so het up before. Back home at the tavern, she'd hardly say 'boo' to a goose."

"Graves ought to have stood firm. Why, even she wouldn't find fault with such a day! It's like rowing on a millpond."

"Well, the woman was ailing. Reckon we were all ailing for a while there!" They chuckled at the memory of how seasickness brought low even the burliest among them.

Beyond the knot of men, Ruth saw Ned and the older boys talking with Uncle Jack while Mr. Smith held the wheel. She picked her way through the crowd until she drew near enough to hear but not actually join the group.

Horace Boardman, who knew the ports of Lake Erie from sailing with his father, was questioning the captain about the rest of their journey.

"Well, my boy, from here on out, we're both charting a new course." Uncle Jack laughed. "On my usual run

74

from Buffalo I only go as far as Cleveland."

"But you went all the way to Illinois to stake your claim, didn't you?"

"Sure, but remember shipping started late this year. I don't think the ice broke up on the lakes until May. When we staked our claim it was still fairly early in the spring. My brother Joe and I had to go overland."

"So you've never sailed Lake Huron or Lake Michigan?"

"Not yet! But don't you worry. My first mate Mr. Smith here has been as far as Green Bay and I have some fine up-to-date charts and maps."

Looking ahead, Horace pointed excitedly to where the river opened into a wide blue bay. "There's Lake Huron!" he called out, but Mr. Smith corrected him.

"That's just Lake St. Clair—a cow pond compared to Lake Huron. We'll be on the other side by supper."

Mr. Smith's prediction proved true, even though the wind died down considerably during the afternoon. The *Telegraph* serenely floated into the marsh that separated the two lakes. Being a small ship with a shallow draft, she ran little risk of being grounded here in the Flats,

St. Clair Flats
A marshy part of the St. Clair River that connects Lake Huron with Lake Erie.

even though heavily laden. Other ships were not so lucky, and Uncle Jack entertained the men at supper with tales he heard from other captains.

Sitting outside watching the sun set, Ruth listened to what a Great Lakes captain would call horror stories. Uncle Jack told them of captains who unloaded every last bit of cargo, removing even sails, chains, and fittings, to lighten the ship enough to float out of the mud, drawing gales of laughter from the men in the cabin. The children waiting for supper listened through the open door and laughed along even though their stomachs were rumbling. The stories encouraged the men to sit overlong at the table, but nobody could tell a funny story like Uncle Jack!

By the time Ruth ate and helped clean up supper, velvety black surrounded the ship on all sides, relieved only by the stars spilling across the sky. Since it was the new moon, not even a sliver gleamed to reflect in the black water. The raucous stories from supper dwindled in the hushed darkness. People on deck talked in low voices, if at all, and even the sails quieted as the wind stilled.

Ruth stood leaning over the rail, staring into the darkness. If she could just open her eyes wide enough, she felt sure she would see something out there. But the dark just went on and on. Mariah joined her at the rail, and they stood together for a few moments before Mariah broke the silence.

"It's so still tonight! Can't hardly believe we had such a storm just a couple days ago!"

"I know. It feels somehow—strange."

"Maybe we're under a spell. Maybe the whole world has suddenly stopped and the people on this ship are the only ones not bewitched. If we went onshore with a lantern, we would see bullfrogs frozen in mid leap. And raccoons stuck to the tree trunks like statues!" The girls giggled and the uneasiness passed.

"How is your ma and baby Susan?" Ruth asked.

"Tolerable well. They're both asleep already. Ma says birthing tuckers a baby out, but that Susan will be making plenty of noise in a few days when she's rested up."

"Then it's good your Ma is resting, too." Ruth laughed. "I reckon birthing tuckered her out just as much!"

Mariah smiled, but she seemed preoccupied. "Ma's tired, all right, but I think her spirits are low, too. Susan's a fine, healthy baby, but..." she trailed off uncomfortably. Ruth waited, quietly encouraging, and Mariah tried again to finish her thought.

"I know Ma and Pa are fond of all of us, but five daughters! Ma was so hoping to give Pa a son this time. Of course we have Allen, but he's been with his grandparents ever since his ma died. We don't hardly know him yet. Even Pa has only seen him once or twice since he was little." Mariah sighed. "We were hoping for our own boy."

Both girls stared out over the black water. "How did Allen's ma die?" Ruth asked.

"Birthing her second baby—Oh!" Mariah stopped short, guilt-stricken. "The baby died, too," she finally finished in a small voice.

Ruth waited, quietly and without movement. As she had noticed before, not cluttering up the silence with a pack of words seemed to make everything much clearer. Before long, Mariah gave Ruth's arm a squeeze and turned to go. "I think I'll go check on Ma and Susan before I turn in," she said.

Ruth stayed at the rail for a few moments longer, wondering where Daidí and Henry and the livestock were at that moment. Daidí would enjoy being on the ship tonight while it was so calm. He wasn't much of a sailor. Very different from Uncle Jack and Uncle Joe! They were born to be lake captains like their father before them. No, Daidí was much better with oxen and horses. Bringing the cattle overland, that was his proper part of this journey. Still, she missed him. With a little sigh, Ruth returned to the cabin to lie down next to Cordelia and sleep.

The weather overnight was so mild that Ruth slept soundly. Bright sunlight streamed in through the open door and the children were willingly shooed out onto the deck while breakfast was being prepared.

The *Telegraph* floated on a thin ribbon of water that wound through a broad sea of tall grass. A distance behind, the wide blue of Lake St. Clair glittered. Ruth was surprised to still see the St. Clair since they entered the Flats before sundown the night before. Surely they should have traveled farther away by now. She puzzled over this, watching red-winged blackbirds swooping and diving among the reeds until two squabbling birds caused a small patch to shake violently while all around the grasses remained perfectly still.

Ruth looked both forward and aft, but far as she could see the *Telegraph* was surrounded by green as motionless as a painting. Not the slightest breeze rippled through the grass. She looked up at the masts, spread with full sail, but drooping and silent. The *Telegraph* was becalmed.

After the men breakfasted, they gathered on deck to discuss the situation. Waiting for their meal, Mariah and Ruth drew near and listened while they kept an eye on the younger children. Uncle Jack assured everyone it was hardly uncommon to lose the wind in the St. Clair Flats, but that they would continue to make some progress.

"And if we get a piece of luck, maybe a steamer will overtake us and we can prevail on her to haul us through," Uncle Joe put in. "In the meantime, gentlemen, I suggest we ask Captain Jack here to lower the scow and let us go ashore until the wind picks up. Any of you fellows good enough

Scow

A flat bottomed boat used to haul freight.

79

fishermen to catch us some dinner?"

The children were wild to go ashore too, and hurried through their meal and chores. The scow had already been back and forth through the marsh several times, and Dick, the crewman at the oars, was hot and thirsty when he drew up to the *Telegraph* where they waited anxiously.

"Go on with you!" Dick growled. "I'm not rowing out there again." Every eager face fell.

"Please, Dick!" Loring begged, "Take us ashore!"

"We'll pull the oars!" Ned added.

"I'll fetch you some of the tea left from breakfast!" Mariah offered.

Dick mopped his sunburned neck with his handkerchief and squinted up at the faces peering through the rails. He stuffed the handkerchief back into his waistband with deliberate slowness before replying.

"Very well. Fetch the tea and get leave from your mamas. Lively, now! I won't wait more than two minutes!"

The children scattered like pill bugs when their rock is picked up. In a remarkably short time, Dick had his tea, Ned and Loring were at the oars, and mothers were calling down last warnings to the little boat below. Ruth and Mariah each had a brood of young chicks to mind, but that was a small price to pay for being allowed onshore. Best of all, Mother offered to look after Mrs. Sisson, baby Susan and little Clarissa, who was really still a baby herself, giving Mariah unexpected freedom.

Dick directed the boys to a hillock of grass already trampled down by previous landings. As they all clambered out, he warned them that the water level was high this season, and the Flats particularly marshy.

"You keep the little ones out of the mud, or they'll be sucked in faster than a frog swallows a fly. Don't be going too far inland, though, or you'll lose sight of the ship. Move up the channel, 'cause if she catches a breeze, the ship will pass you right by. And listen for my hail. When the Captain says it's time to come aboard, you come!"

The youngsters nodded solemnly, but could hardly keep their feet still, so eager were they to escape. Finally, Dick took out his black handkerchief to mop his brow one more time, and pushed off from the hillock.

Ned and Loring took off into the tall grass instantly with the other boys close behind. Having the shortest legs, George trailed them, shouting at their backs: "Hey, fellows! Wait for me!"

Amos tried to bolt as well, but wise to his ways, Ruth grabbed him by the back of his braces just as he turned. "Mother said you were not to tag after Ned and get lost! You're to stay where I can keep an eye on you." His eight-

Braces
Straps that cross over the shoulders and are attached by buttons to a man's trousers to keep them from falling off.

year-old sensibilities greatly injured, Amos gloomily trudged after the two older girls and their band of younger sisters.

The girls and Amos followed the trail left by previous parties. The grass and occasional mud squishing between their toes felt deliciously cool with the sun hot on their shoulders. Before long, Ruth saw where the older boys had turned off, going deeply inland, directly where they were told not to go.

"Ned's going to get those boys in trouble!" Ruth thought. "Well, they're old enough to know better! Would serve them right if they missed Dick's call!"

Amos lingered at the gap in the tall grass, but turned away as soon as Ruth opened her mouth to warn him against trying to escape. "All right, all right! Don't get your pantaloons in a knot!" he growled.

The scenery became monotonous with reeds as tall as Ruth's head surrounding them. Closer to the water the grassy hillocks quickly gave way to deep black mud, but on the other side marshland stretched farther than Ruth thought prudent to walk. Ella, the smallest of the group, started tiring first. Mariah jollied Ella along even though her own cheeks were red and the tendrils of hair on her forehead damp.

Over the tops of the reeds, the children could see a canopy of green. Renewed, they doubled their pace and were soon rewarded by a small shady copse of willow on a fairly firm embankment. Although a favorite sunning spot for a family of ducks, the birds noisily surrendered ownership, gliding out onto the channel. Flopping down under the trees, Ruth and Mariah untied their bonnets and pushed up their sleeves.

Although it was more pleasant in the shade, no breeze cooled the children's hot faces. Quacking protests from the ducks faded away and the only sound was the droning of dragonflies. The younger ones couldn't sit still for long, and soon were at the edge of the water looking for raccoon footprints in the mud and kicking water at each other.

"As long as you're wet," Ruth called, "you might as well look for clams. We can take them back to the ship for supper." Amos found some sturdy sticks and they began digging. Ruth and Mariah lay back against the trunks of a couple of willow trees and watched with their eyes half closed.

"Do you think you'll miss Ohio?" Mariah asked lazily. "I know I'll miss New York. It was only half a day's journey into town. Pa sometimes would bring us sugar candy or calico when he came back. I wonder how far we'll be from town at the new settlement."

"Uncle Joe says you can reach Fort Dearborn in a long day's ride. Uncle Jack says, 'Maybe so, but why would you want to?'"

Mariah giggled, followed by a deep sigh. "Doesn't sound like Detroit, does it? No sugar candy or new calico for us. At least not in the beginning. But we'll all have so much land that we'll be very wealthy and build two-story houses with real glass windows and send for our calico and candy from New York." She sat up suddenly. "Is your brother Ned old enough to homestead his own land? Maybe I'll marry him."

Ruth laughed at her and rolled onto her stomach, keeping Cordelia and Amos in view. With her chin in her hands, she thought about how quickly the life she had always known was changing. The farm where she was born and raised was so many miles behind with a new family living there now. Once they reached the settlement, Sally Ann and Henry would stake their own claim, maybe Ned, too. As the oldest child at home, Ruth expected new responsibilities, but for how long? In just a few years, she might have a Henry and a homestead of her own.

But for today, she was just Ruth Eliza Murray given a perfect summer afternoon. "Come on!" she said, pulling Mariah to her feet. "Let's look for clams."

Crayfish
Little lobster-like crustaceans found in fresh water streams.

The girls tucked their skirts up into their waistbands and soon were knee-deep in squishy mud and cool water. They found a good number of clams, as well as some crayfish, and tied them all up in Amos's shirt. When they tired of digging, everyone gathered under the trees to eat the biscuits and salt pork Mother gave them before they left the ship. Stomachs full, the little girls dozed in the grass like puppies.

The late afternoon air was still and hot and even Amos was content to sit on a fallen log and dangle a fishing line into the water. Mariah embroidered tales of the hardships her family braved over the past winter, but eventually she, too, fell silent. Ruth didn't even realize her eyes were closed when a crashing in the brush behind her startled her awake.

Loring and some of the other boys burst through the reeds, bug-eyed and panting and all talking at once.

"Thank Providence we found you!"

"You've got to come—quick!"

"Oh, he got it bad!"

Fully awake, Ruth scrambled to her feet. "Is it Ned? What's happened? Take me to him!" She pulled Cordelia up and called to Amos to follow. Loring had already disappeared back into the tall grass and was shouting over his shoulder to hurry.

Ruth By Lake And Prairie

CHAPTER 8

SUNNY DAYS ON LAKE HURON

hat's happened?" Ruth demanded again as she followed Allen, George and the other boys down the rough trail.

"Bees! They got Ned real bad," Allen explained. "We saw the bees and followed them, and we could see where they were crawling into this big crack in a tree. It was real high, but Ned said he could climb it. And he did, but just when he got to where we thought the honeycomb was, the branch he was standing on broke—"

"Oh, he was real high! He would've broken his arm or something for sure!" George interrupted. "But he grabbed for the tree and sort of slid down the trunk."

"But he grabbed where the crack was and some of it broke off and it made the bees awful mad!"

The story poured out in a jumble of anxious voices, the boys breaking in on each other as they tried to explain what happened.

"They were swarming him all the way down the tree!"

"And his shirt and trousers got all ripped up as he slid down!"

"They were stinging and stinging, and he was hollering

and hollering—"

"And you ran away," Ruth accused. The boys subsided sheepishly. "Well, how much farther?" she asked.

From up ahead, Loring called back that they were nearly there. Ruth quickened her pace, dragging along poor little Cordelia, who was barely able to keep up. The forest of reeds opened up to a meadow of grass and flowers about waist high. A stand of trees grew on the other side. About midway through the meadow, Loring's head bobbed above the seed heads as he hurried along. Suddenly he stopped and bent down, disappearing into the grass, before popping back up and waving his arms.

"Over here!" he called. "He's over here!"

Dropping Cordelia's hand, Ruth raced over. Ned was sitting on the ground, cursing with vigor when they got there, but Ruth could see his eyes were bright and wet. She suspected he might have indulged in an unmanly cry before they found him.

Ned's face and arms were red, swollen, and lumpy, and his chest was bloodied beneath the shreds of his shirt. Ruth kneeled down beside him, just looking him over without speaking. Ned met her eyes with a shamefaced grin. At least Ruth wasn't the type to scold like Sally Ann would. "I'm okay," he protested. "Nothing that won't heal."

Ruth shook her head, but managed a smile of her own. "You weren't that handsome before, Ned Murray! Now look at you! Come down to the water and wash up.

We can poultice the stings so they don't ache so bad." She helped him up. By that time, Mariah and the girls had caught up and they all turned around, following the trodden-down grass back to the channel.

Once there, Ned jumped into the water, clothes and all. He yelped as the water washed over his scraped chest, but admitted that the coolness eased the bee stings a bit. Hanging on to Amos's fishing log, he floated to keep his feet from getting sucked into the muddy bottom.

"What kind of poultice can you put on out here?" Ned asked.

"If you have your tobacco with you, you can chew some up and put it on the stings."

Ned snorted. "It doesn't hurt enough to waste my tobacco! Have you got any other ideas?

Ruth considered. "Well, yes! I've got one Gran told me about. Come on out of the water."

Once Ned was back on shore, Ruth sat him down and sent the children to grab handfuls of thick, black mud. The little ones particularly enjoyed slathering it on Ned's welts, and since he had so many, he was nearly black all over before they were done.

"Now sit here in the sun until the mud dries. It will draw the poison out, and the itching will go away," Ruth promised.

At first, Ned complained that the drying mud itched almost as much as the bee stings. He was amusing

Cordelia by flexing his muscles to crack the muddy shell when they heard a "Halloo!" from upriver as the scow rounded a bend in the channel. Ned waved, sending shards of mud flying, and the children gathered up the clams and other treasures they had found.

"What sort of bogey do you have there?" Dick called, laughing at Ned. "You'll not be coming aboard like that, my boy." While the scow made its way to the riverbank, Ned jumped back into the water to rinse off.

The children climbed into the boat, eagerly relating Ned's story while the crewman headed for the *Telegraph*. The ship had caught a bit of breeze during the bee rescue and passed them by. Ned and Loring pulled against the current, but it was such a wide, shallow expanse that they had little trouble, and soon drew alongside the ship.

That evening, everyone was in a merry mood. Those who remained onboard were rested and relaxed, while those who had gone ashore proudly displayed the fish and clams they brought back. The chowder prepared for supper that night was a pleasant change from bacon and beans, and although there was no honey for their ship's biscuit, Ned's story accompanied the meal perfectly.

Perhaps the storms of the previous week had used up all the wind, but only the barest breezes moved the *Telegraph*'s sails during the next few days. Progress up the river was slow, and one day when they passed a lonely farmstead the scow rowed busily back and forth as nearly all the passengers were anxious to escape the monotony onboard.

The old French settler and his Indian wife were just as pleased to have company, and between them all enough English, French, and Ottawa was spoken to ensure a lively conversation. Discovering the Frenchman owned a cow and a calf, a bargain was struck to buy milk to take back on the ship.

"If we take the milk, will the little calf go hungry?" Cordelia asked Ruth anxiously.

"Not at all. Look! He's eating some of that grass by the fence post. He's almost too big to need any milk at all anymore."

While Ruth and Cordelia watched the calf, they heard delighted squeals from the lean-to shed behind them. "Oh, aren't they sweet! Ruth, come see!" Mariah called from inside.

"Kittens!" Cordelia breathed ecstatically, dropping immediately to the straw-covered floor. "Can we bring one onboard? Please?"

"I don't think Uncle Jack would—Oh! Look at the little black one!"

So enraptured were the girls by the kittens' antics, they could hardly bear to leave when Dick hallooed from the scow that the wind was

Lean-To

A shelter with a roof sloping in only one direction, often built up against the wall of another building.

freshening and it was time to come aboard. A long-legged man could still outrun the ship, but at least the breeze stayed steady all evening and into the morning. Captain Naper grew concerned around midday that he had steered the *Telegraph* down a false channel in the marsh. The reeds grew thicker here, nearly blocking the waterway entirely, and he was in serious discussion with his brother Joseph and Mr. Smith when the river suddenly opened up again. By nightfall they were in Delude, where they planned to take on fresh provisions before setting out on the choppy waters of Lake Huron.

To make up for the time lost while they were becalmed in the St. Clair flats, Uncle Jack decided to bypass Saginaw Bay entirely. The *Telegraph* was out of sight of land for nearly two days crossing it, even with a stiff wind.

Allen and George played at pirates much of that time. Amos was thrilled to be allowed to join the game, although he spent most of it bound to the mast as a prisoner of war. Even the younger girls were asked to join in when extra prisoners were needed. Professing to be too old to play, Ned and Loring still swooped down occasionally from the rigging as marauding pirate kings when the children least expected it.

Mariah and Ruth pretended to disdain such rough and tumble playacting, but in truth they spent many hours weaving an elaborate pirate adventure of their own while supposedly minding the little ones. Mariah, of course, thought up most of the tale, encouraged by Ruth's admiration. Sometimes Ruth's practicality compelled her to point out flaws in the story, but Mariah rarely seemed to hear those comments.

"High above the deck, Diana, the Pirate Queen, climbed the rigging, hand over hand. Unable to stop, the two ships crashed full into each! The mast of the Scorpion cracked in two, and the ropes of the rigging snapped, hurtling Diana into the foamy waves! Fortunately, a whale swam by and lifted her on its great back—"

"Are there whales in the South Seas?" Ruth asked mildly. Baby Eunice was starting to fuss in her arms, so Ruth set Eunice down on the deck.

"It was a lost whale," Mariah said, hardly slowing down. "Diana was kind to it on a previous adventure, and it followed her down to the South Seas."

Eunice sat still for a moment, then performed her new trick of tumbling onto her belly so she could pull herself along the deck. Her progress was slow, but she was determined, and Ruth had to step on the hem of Eunice's long dress to keep her from edging any farther away. Thwarted, Eunice tried another direction, creeping as far as her gown would take her. Her flailing reminded Ruth for all the world of the painted turtles she and Ned used to race on the banks of the stream back home.

"Maybe Diana was rescued by a giant turtle. A sailor told Uncle Jack once about giant turtles in the South

Seas."

Mariah considered for a moment and then nodded her head. "A giant sea turtle lifted Diana onto its back. Cannon balls from the two ships slammed into the water all around them! But she gripped the edge of its shell and the giant sea turtle swam away as fast as it could go."

Uncle Joe happened to be passing by as Mariah finished off this latest chapter in the pirate saga. "Giant sea turtle, eh? You know, our next port is called the Land of the Great Turtle. That's what 'Mish-la-mack-in-naw' means in the old native tongue. It's the home of Gitchee Manitou, the Indians' Great Spirit."

"Does Gitchee Manitou live there still?" Mariah asked, entranced.

"Nah—he took himself off when the fur traders moved in. Guess Frenchmen offend him! Now he lives in the Northern Lights, the natives say. But we still call the island Mackinac. And we'll be sailing through the Manitou passage as well. So maybe you'll get a peek at Gitchee Manitou after all!"

The girls eagerly awaited their arrival in Mackinac. A few days later, Uncle Joe kindly pointed out Bois Blanc Island in the distance, which meant they would make Mackinac before sunset. He explained that "bois blanc" was French for "woods of white," and indeed birch trees with peeling white bark crowded the island down to the water line. Rounding this northernmost tip of the Michigan territory, the *Telegraph* fought a stiff headwind, and Mariah despaired of ever reaching the sacred island home of the Gitchee Manitou.

Mackinac

In the upper peninsula of Michigan, the Mackinac Straits is a passage between Lake Huron and Lake Michigan. The British built the fort on Mackinac Island, lost it in the Revolutionary War, and reclaimed it in the War of 1812.

Mackinac Island dashed the dearest hopes of their imaginations, even though they approached it as the sun set in a romantic red sky. Smaller even than Bois Blanc, it looked no more like a great turtle than any other bump of land in the lake, no matter how hard they squinted at it. Long a military fort for both the British and the Americans, it now boasted a bustling port with a brisk trade in beaver pelts and whitefish. Mariah and Ruth could easily see why Gitchee Manitou abandoned his sacred island.

Although disappointed, the girls still went ashore with the other passengers the next morning as the crew took on barrels of salted fish for trade at Fort Dearborn. The families from Ashtabula hiked straight up to the fort, eager to see the site where Ben Naper had been captured by the British during the war in 1812. Ned led the party, escorted by an admiring platoon of boys.

Beaver Hat
Beaver fur was used to make felt which in turn was used to make extremely popular hats in the 18th and 19th centuries, nearly wiping out the beaver population.

"My Uncle Ben was a mate on the Salina when war was declared," Ned boasted. "She regularly carried a cargo of over a hundred thousand dollars in beaver skins in her run from Mackinac to Buffalo. She was quite a prize for the British!"

"Did the British board her, like pirates?" Allen asked.

"Didn't have to," Ned replied. "They snuck onto the island and captured the fort. Then when the ships came into harbor, they sailed right into enemy territory. There were passengers onboard, too, civilians and children. Those who wouldn't take the oath for England were sent back to Detroit. And when Detroit fell, the Salina was captured again!"

"Again!" one of the boys exclaimed.

"Yep! That's when Uncle Ben decided he wasn't taking any more from the British! He went back to Ashtabula and joined the army, along with my dad. I wasn't born yet, and Sally Ann was just a baby."

"Did Captain Jack and Captain Joe go into the army, too?" Allen asked.

"Nah, they weren't old enough. Still wet behind the ears—like you!" Ned knocked Allen's hat back with a meaty fist, but Allen didn't mind. As the object of growing hero worship, any attention from Ned was welcomed.

Ruth, Mariah, and the children tagged along on the visit to the fort, but their interest waned far sooner than that of the boys. Drifting back towards the pier, they found enough early raspberries in a sunny patch along the edge of the forest to distract them. Risking thorns and scratched arms, they quickly filled Amos' straw hat, even though they ate two berries for every one they brought back to the ship.

The next morning the *Telegraph* cast off from Mackinac and sailed into the third and last Great Lake of her journey. From here on would be real wilderness, with very few ports of call or even homesteads along the shore. The uncles spent several hours at the fort before casting off talking over their route with men who had already made the trip to Green Bay and Fort Dearborn. Armed with advice and charts, they felt sure of the way.

Even though they would have to contend with prevailing winds from the west, Uncle Jack decided to follow the eastern shoreline rather than the longer western route. The weather continued clear and pleasant, and Ruth and Mariah often wished they could sleep out on deck as their brothers did. At night, the arch of sky swept high overhead and merged with the far horizon. Lit by a full moon, the lake reflected like a mirror so that the ship seemed suspended in a cloud of stars.

During the day, no clouds softened the summer sun, and even though a stiff breeze fanned them constantly, the glare and heat were often overwhelming. It became a favorite pastime to wash laundry since it kept the children occupied as well as cooled off. Normally washing was an unpleasant chore women performed rarely. Soap making took a long time, and the lye in it burned your skin when it splashed. Large kettles of water needed to be filled and boiled, and the clothes scrubbed, rinsed, and hung over bushes.

Laundry on the ship was much simplified. With just the one small stove onboard, boiling water with lye soap was deemed unnecessary. Instead, they washed in cold water like the Indians. The crew provided a bucket tethered with rope. The children dropped the bucket overboard, let it fill, and then pulled it back onboard, much more fun than hauling water from a stream. Wet clothes, whether intentionally or accidentally drenched, dried quickly in the sun and wind on deck, although weights were needed to keep shirts from blowing overboard.

The *Telegraph* turned south and made her way down the lake, mainly following the shoreline. Since the weather was so fine, Captain Jack cut across some broad bays to make up time lost early in the trip. He carefully observed landmarks and compared them to his charts and the notes he made at the fort. Not far from the biggest bay lay the treacherous Manitou Passage, and the crew wanted ample warning to navigate its shallow, rocky waters.

Mariah and Ruth watched eagerly for the Manitou Passage as well. Also supposedly sacred islands, maybe here they would find the Great Spirit Manitou. The children never tired of hearing how the islands were created in compassion by the Manitou. Having heard the tale once from Dick, Mariah retold it to the younger ones with her own imaginative touches. She really did it remarkably well, Ruth thought, not for the first time wondering how people made up things in their heads like that.

"Flaming trees crashed to the ground behind them as they ran toward the lake! The mother bear nudged her cubs into the water, but the fire crept ever closer to the shore, steaming and hissing as the waves rolled in. They were surrounded by flames!"

Cordelia wrung her hands together. "What will they do?" she exclaimed.

Mariah's voice dropped and she leaned closer. "There's only one thing they can do—swim across the lake! The mother bear splashed into the water and set off for the other shore. The little cubs tried to keep up with her, but they were too small and too weary. She grabbed one in her mouth and helped it along, but then the other fell behind, and she had to go back for him. She paddled and pushed and pulled, but soon even she was struggling to stay afloat. Finally, exhausted, she dragged herself up on the beach, gasping for air."

With perfect timing, Mariah paused and looked down at the little faces, slack-jawed and big-eyed, before continuing in her most dramatic voice. "But when she looked around, she was alone. Her little cubs had tired and were lost beneath the waves."

Out of the corner of her eye, Ruth noticed that Aunt Almeda hovered just behind, watching her children and listening to the story. Unlike Aunt Betsy, who seemed to gather people around her, Aunt Almeda preferred observing from the edge of a group.

"The Spirit Manitou looked down at the poor mother bear and took pity on her. He threw a blanket of sleep over her so that she could stop grieving and finally rest. A great mountain of sand stands on the shore to this day where she sleeps."

"And the poor little cubs?" Cordelia asked.

"The Manitou placed two islands in the water where the baby bears drowned. Those islands are sacred to him. The passage between the islands and the shore he made treacherous as a warning to those who pass by to show proper respect. That's why Captain Naper is watching his charts so carefully. He doesn't want the *Telegraph* and all of us on her to draw the Manitou's wrath!"

The children gasped, and Ruth heard a low chuckle

behind her. "Jack is promised plenty of cooperation when he does navigate the Passage," Aunt Almeda smiled. "But I'm not sure how well these children will sleep tonight!"

CHAPTER 9

FEAR AND CELEBRATION

Aunt Almeda's prophecy proved true. Although Captain Naper assured them that he would not attempt to maneuver the Manitou Passage in the dark, every creak of the ship or flutter of the sail sounded ominous that night, and even Ruth, who told herself she had no imagination, found it difficult to relax and close her eyes.

The next day, Dick pointed out the two islands where the cubs were supposed to have drowned. Ruth and Mariah gazed eagerly across the water, fully expecting to see some awful spirit, painted and feathered, rise from the forests. With a favoring wind and the *Telegraph*'s shallow draft, Captain Jack easily passed through the rocky strait, and the islands receded quickly and uneventfully.

Mariah turned from the rail and heaved a sigh. "I guess I knew it truly was just a story for children," she said ruefully.

Ruth always considered herself a no-nonsense sort of person, but secretly she was disappointed, too. "Maybe the Manitou moved away, like Uncle Joe told us. Maybe he only appears to the Indians."

"Maybe. Well, shall we practice our recitation?"

The rest of the evening until supper, the girls whispered together on a sunny patch of the deck. The Fourth of July was only a week away, and they were preparing a recitation of Francis Scott Key's poem "The Star-Spangled Banner" for the celebration. Ruth knew nearly the whole poem by heart, and was teaching it line by line to Mariah who made up words to fit what Ruth couldn't remember.

Originally they planned to recite the verses in turns, but no matter how Mariah coached and encouraged, Ruth's placid narration just couldn't keep up with Mariah's more animated version. Ruth was demoted to providing the accompanying sounds, but when Mariah decided that even Ruth's bomb noises lacked spirit, Ruth settled into her more familiar roles as prompter and audience.

Other small knots of passengers debated and rehearsed on the deck until a sudden shower sent them running for cover. The rain didn't last long, but signaled an abrupt drop in temperature and a bone-chilling dampness. By the time she turned in for the night, Ruth was glad to be sleeping in the cabin with the females.

The next few days continued cold. White-crested waves smacked against the hull. While strong, the wind was for the most part contrary, and the *Telegraph* did not make good time. Captain Naper and the crew struggled to keep her far from shore. To run aground now would be disastrous. Mainly wilderness from Mackinac to Fort Dearborn, they couldn't count on rescue from land or lake.

Occasionally a squall overtook them, and then the passengers hunkered down in the cabin or in the hold until it passed. Ruth couldn't claim that they ever got used to storms, but the panic and desperation felt between Cleveland and Detroit was deadened to a numb acceptance.

The days ran together in wearying monotony. On the starboard side of the ship stretched an unvarying vista of water and sky the color of lead. On the port side, forbiddingly dark pine forests and black rocks ran up and down the coast. All alone, the little ship fought her way down the lake.

The cold and damp soaked into their clothes and bedding. Ruth felt clammy and chilled all the time, and longed to bask in the sun like a turtle on a log. Poor Gran huddled against the little stove in the cabin all day, her shawl drawn around tightly, but still she shivered, knitting with icy fingers.

Then one night as they were preparing to sleep, Ruth heard thunder across the lake. It grew louder, and Ruth wondered how long before it overtook them. She listened and counted, and soon realized that instead of drawing nearer, the squall was passing them to the north. The rumbling faded away as she fell asleep, and when she woke the cabin sparkled with sunshine.

The children hurried through breakfast. Today was the Fourth of July, and after days of grayness, the passengers eagerly looked forward to celebrating. Giggles and bustle broke out all over the ship. Packs were rifled through, workbaskets raided. Kitchen utensils went missing, making dinner preparations even more difficult than cooking onboard already was. Over it all, the summer sun smiled down in friendly fashion.

Finally all was ready. Uncle Jack called everyone to order from a podium hastily contrived from a couple of crates. When the passengers gathered around and shushed the little ones, Mariah's father, Mr. Sisson, led them all in a long prayer. In his gruff voice, Mr. Sisson expressed thankfulness for their safety thus far, and pleaded for their success and happiness in their new homes as well. Heartfelt "Amens!" resounded from the crowd as he finished.

Next, Uncle Joe stepped up on the crates, a creased paper in his hands. He shook it out and rattled it importantly before sternly looking out at the audience from beneath his bushy eyebrows. Silence fell across the ship.

"When in the course of human events," he boomed, "it becomes necessary for one people to dissolve the political bands which have connected them with another and to assume among the powers of the earth, the separate and equal station to which—"

Uncle Joe continued to read the Declaration of

Independence, but Ruth's mind wandered. Many times in past summers, Daidí had read the same words on the square in Ashtabula. While Uncle Joe had a fine, strong voice that carried well over the rustling of sails and creaking of ropes, Daidí played his voice like an instrument. Not nearly as loud, it still reached the farthest edge of a crowd because people quieted and drew near the better to hear his beautiful words. Ruth wondered if Daidí would recite for Henry tonight at their own small celebration on the prairie.

Ruth was called back to the present, realizing that Uncle Joe was nearing the end. "We mutually pledge to each other our Lives, our Fortunes and our sacred Honor!" he finished triumphantly, waving the paper over his head. Hearty cheers went up from the men and boys. Uncle Joe stepped down and helped Sally Ann on top of the crate. She stood tall and slim and lifted her chin, just like Daidí had taught her, while she sang.

"Hail, Columbia! Happy land! Hail, ye heroes, heav'n-born band!" When she had sung the last note, the people cheered so loud and long that to please them Sally Ann sang it again. Ruth clapped as enthusiastically as the rest, but a wistful voice sighed in her head. What did it feel like to have a gift that prompted such noisy admiration?

Other songs and recitations followed. Mariah climbed atop the makeshift stage when her turn came, her head barely visible above the throng. Mariah's eyes were just a

107

little too wide and she licked her lips more than once. Now that was a feeling with which Ruth was very familiar. Fortunately, at that moment Mariah saw Ruth, too. Encouraged, she began to recite. With every line Mariah's voice grew stronger, and by the second verse, her hands fluttered in illustration of "the breeze...as it fitfully blows" just like she practiced it.

"And the star-spangled banner in triumph shall wave o'er the land of the free and the home of the brave!" Mariah concluded to whistles and cheers. She curtsied elegantly and jumped down from the crate. Making her way through the crowd while Uncle Joe and Uncle Jack sang a comical song about a sailor and a mermaid, Mariah collapsed on Ruth's shoulder.

"I've never recited before so many people before! Feel my hands—they're just shaking!"

"Mariah, you were wonderful! Did you hear how they all applauded? I could never stand up there and give a speech."

"I almost couldn't either! Thank the heavens you were there. As soon as I saw you, I knew everything would be all right." She gave Ruth an affectionate squeeze.

After a couple more songs, dinner was pronounced ready, and the men went into the cabin. On deck, the girls practiced dance steps with the younger children while hungrily awaiting their turn. Due to the rough weather and the restrictions of the little stove, there would be no fresh bread or pie, but hot cornmeal mush with a generous ladle of molasses on top made a sweet hasty pudding that everyone looked forward to.

While the children were enjoying their meal, they could hear the men joking and whispering out on deck as they readied themselves for their Fourth of July presentation. Originally, the men had planned a parade on shore, but when no safe harbor could be found, Captain Naper decided to just drop anchor near a natural rocky breakwater and hold the Fourth celebrations onboard. Instead of a parade, the men and boys would be performing a sort of tableau.

Dinner finished and cleared away, the passengers found perches on crates, wagon boxes, and even up on the cabin roof or in the rigging. Space was cleared for a stage in front of the cabin door. After much hooting and calling from the eager audience, Mr. Sisson came through the doorway. He held up his hands until the crowd silenced.

"My dear ladies and esteemed gentlemen! On this, the celebration of our independence, it is traditional to honor our forefathers who stood up to tyranny and oppression, and created this free nation—our beloved United States of America!" Cheers interrupted him.

"And so, ladies and gentlemen, in tribute to those brave souls who served in our armed forces during the War for Independence, I give you New York State's finest regiment—the Dutchess County Minute Men!"

Wild applause and laughter broke out as a troop of

men marched through the cabin door. They sported the oddest assortment of clothes, from Captain Naper's worn rain cloak to Mrs. Babbit's fullest petticoat. Some had one trouser leg rolled up or had swapped shoes so a different boot adorned each foot.

Little Mr. Peck wrapped himself in the longest jacket on the ship while broad Mr. Boardman squeezed into the smallest. On their heads were Granny Naper's mob cap, Amos' berry-stained straw, bowls, baskets, and even a chamber pot! Each "hat" was adorned with a gull feather.

Uncle Jack came striding out next, commander of the ragged brigade. With his felt hat pinned into a three-cornered shape and Gran's gray wool yarn arranged underneath as a wig, he looked just like an etching of General Washington. Drawing his sword, which turned out to be the kitchen ladle, Uncle Jack called the men to attention. "Prepare for inspection!" he bawled.

Mobcap
A puffy, frilly cap worn indoors by women in the late 1700's and early 1800's.

He sauntered up and down the ranks, making jokes until Ruth's sides ached from laughter. Finally, Uncle Jack commanded them to "Present arms!" The men shouldered brooms, mops, and even a fiddle bow before executing a comical marching drill that had them tripping over each other. They capped their performance with a lusty rendition of "Yankee Doodle" and took their bows.

110

Not to be outdone, the younger boys, led by Allen and Loring, performed their own tableau—a reenactment of the War of 1812. Consisting mainly of noise, wrestling, and dramatic death scenes, Mr. Sisson shortened the war by a battle

Three-Cornered Hat or Tricorn

A hat with its broad brim pinned up on three sides to look triangular. Popular until 1800.

or two and led the audience in a few songs.

As the sun set, the menfolk passed around whiskey and blackstrap molasses, and between choruses they drank toasts to the President and to the flag, then to the Army and to the Navy. They toasted each of the original thirteen states that broke away from England, and then toasted the newest states. By the time someone called a toast "To the fair sex," the women were settling into the cabin for the night with the littlest ones.

Still too wound up to sleep, Ruth and Mariah left the men to their tobacco and politics. They hung on the rail and searched the sky for shooting stars. The sun had gone down in glorious scarlet among the hulking mass of clouds moving in from the west, but the sky was still clear and sparkling directly overhead.

Mariah pointed suddenly. "There! By the North Star!" Ruth barely caught the quick streak of light before it faded. Ruth wondered if Daidí and Henry were lying on their blankets watching the stars tonight, if they had

111

seen this one arc across the sky.

"Isn't it odd," Ruth said dreamily, "that we're looking at the same stars that we used to see back east? And even when we get to our new homes, we'll look up into the sky at night, and the same stars will be there. Just like they always have been!" She flung out her arm in an uncharacteristically dramatic gesture, but stopped short. A low rumble of thunder rolled across the lake.

Lost in her own daydream, it took a moment for Mariah to notice Ruth's tension. "What's wrong?" she asked.

"Out there!" Ruth whispered, her hand still suspended in midair. Mariah turned to the north, where Ruth's eyes were fixed.

Far away over the lake, past the distant shoreline that jutted into the water, and maybe as far away as Mackinac, an unearthly glow reached into the sky. Ghostly white tinged with the palest of greens, the glow seemed to fold back on itself like a sheet blowing in the wind rather than radiate from a source. What was left of the waning moon was already overwhelmed by the approaching storm clouds, and the color looked nothing like the reflection of a forest fire.

While they watched, too awed to speak, the wind freshened and blew straight in their faces. Thunder rumbled again, and two smaller pale streaks of light brightened near the first one. Mariah gasped.

"It's the Manitou! And the drowned bear cubs!"

112

Ruth shivered, but was unable to tear her eyes away from the strange lights rippling on the distant horizon. The two smaller objects seemed to catch up to the larger one, joining together in a stunning flare of otherworldly

Northern Lights

A natural phenomenon displaying lights in the sky in many different colors and shapes. Centered on the magnetic north pole, they are rarely seen in the southern United States.

green. Frozen in place, the girls gaped until a sudden bolt of lightning and an explosion of thunder startled them into crying out.

Rain blew in cold and hard, and as the girls dashed toward the cabin, the green glow disappeared behind dark, rolling storm clouds.

Chapter 10

The Last Days Afloat

Storms raged for hours. Ruth and Mariah huddled together whispering well into the night before finally falling into an exhausted sleep. Tuckered out from the Fourth of July celebrations and deceived by the lack of sunshine, everyone overslept in the morning, including the crew. Captain Naper decided to wait out the weather and remained anchored, giving the morning a sluggish start.

As Mariah and Ruth went about their regular routine, the events of the previous night felt uncomfortably fanciful. "It was just Northern Lights," Ruth kept telling herself, "Even if it was out of season." But didn't Uncle Joe say the Manitou went to live in the Northern Lights? Ruth couldn't help remembering, but by unspoken agreement the ghostly lights were never again mentioned between them.

When the crew was ready and a lull between storms appeared, the *Telegraph* weighed anchor and continued along the Lake Michigan shoreline. Progress was slow, however. Captain Naper sailed cautiously through the unfamiliar waters, and the ship was often idled by contrary winds and heavy rain.

The days of inactivity irritated Uncle Joe the most. He calculated and recalculated the earliest date they might arrive at the settlement and how many weeks remained in the growing season. Putting in a crop yet this summer was essential to their survival over the winter, and the weather had already proven unreliable. What if the rains finally stopped just when they were ready to plant? What if they didn't stop and the seedlings washed away or rotted in the ground? Ruth was old enough to remember the hardships of a lean winter. She watched Uncle Joe reading his almanac and studying his figures and wished she could encourage the weather to cooperate.

Almanac

A type of book published every year since the 15th century that predicts weather, phases of the moon, tides and other information useful to farmers.

Once, he looked up while deep in thought and stared at her for a full two minutes before he actually saw her. An apologetic grin finally relaxed his ruddy face. "Why, if it isn't Miss Ruth Eliza!" he laughed. "Watching me so seriously! Come now, you're too young and pretty to look so solemn!"

Muscular, blunt and friendly, Uncle Joe was a favorite with Ned when the *Telegraph* put in at Ashtabula harbor, but since Ruth rarely saw him, she was a little shy. Still, hearing herself declared "pretty" surprised a smile to her lips.

"That's better!" Uncle Joe approved. "You should smile more often. Your aunt Almeda tells me you are a great help to her and the other females in minding the children while on the ship. She has every confidence in your capabilities."

Ruth blushed at the unexpected praise. "Thank you, Uncle," she stammered. Indicating the almanac and notes in his lap, she tried turning the conversation. "Is the weather going to improve?"

"Well, the almanac doesn't commit itself to more than 'unseasonably cool and wet,' which it certainly has been! No early winter is threatened, but it looks to be a cold and long one. If Mr. Scott has managed to clear the ten acres we agreed on, there should still be ample time to grow a fine crop of rutabagas. How will you like eating rutabagas all winter?"

Ruth looked down at her hands in confusion. No one could be excited by the threat of rutabagas all winter! But how was she to answer him without appearing rude? Uncle Joe interrupted her hesitation with a deep bellow of laughter.

Rutabaga
A root vegetable like a turnip.

"Poor Ruth! I have put you in an uncomfortable spot. I know you would not for the world injure my feelings with your true opinion of rutabagas!" He grew serious again. "It may

117

well be a difficult winter this year, but every year after this will only add to our prosperity and happiness. The land is good and cheap and plentiful. We are well prepared and hard working. Together we will build a community that will stand as a model for others as they move westward."

Uncle Joe squinted into the sun as if he could already see this new settlement on the far horizon. Armed with his books and his notes, his broad shoulders and his callused hands, Ruth believed that he would truly do just as he said. She glanced around the ship. All these people! They left their homes and friends to travel cheek by jowl in this stinking ship on a stormy lake. They believed, too.

Recalled from his distant vision, Uncle Joe carefully folded up his notes. "But right now," he chuckled, "we just need to get the *Telegraph* to Fort Dearborn!"

For nearly two weeks the travelers hadn't seen a settlement, a homestead, or even an Indian village, nothing since setting sail from Mackinac. Occasionally a wisp of smoke was spotted above the treetops, or a couple of native men in canoes watched them pass, but for the most part, the *Telegraph* sailed alone.

Headed now almost due west, the crew struggled constantly against the prevailing winds and fitful weather which delayed their progression. Every morning Ned climbed to the top of the rigging to try for a glimpse of Fort Dearborn. Every evening before she went to bed,

Ruth strained to see lantern lights in the darkness. And lately, the darkness seemed especially overwhelming.

With the new moon arriving and frequent clouds blocking even the starlight, darkness wrapped around the little ship every night like a heavy blanket. The wind died down, becalming them, and the usual sounds of flapping sails and creaking ropes quieted as well. No rustling of leaves or peeping of frogs reached them from the shore, so silence weighed uncommonly heavy on the *Telegraph*'s passengers. They found themselves conversing in whispers after the sun set and went early to bed.

One morning while Ruth finished her breakfast, she heard Ned shouting from out on deck. A swell of voices jabbered excitedly, and all the children in the cabin rushed for the door at once. Their parents crowded on the port side of the ship, pointing and exclaiming.

Ned was climbing up in the rigging, and Ruth called to him.

"Ned! What's happened? What do you see?"

"Looks to be Fort Dearborn! We made it!"

The children cheered and scrambled to see for themselves. Allen, Loring, and some of the other boys pulled themselves atop the wagon boxes for a better view. Ruth and Mariah tried to join the crowd at the rail, but Mother said: "Stay here! Do you want the ship to roll over?" They stayed with her by the wagons, but stretched themselves as tall as they could. Cordelia begged to be picked up for a look, too.

Ruth caught a glimpse between the ladies' bonnets. The shore was still a long way off, but there, nestled in a long line of trees, was a huge timbered fort surrounded by cabins just like a hen with her chicks.

"It's still too far, Cordelia," Ruth assured her, teetering on tiptoe for another peek. Mother and the aunts were seated regally around the cargo hatch, apparently indifferent to the noisy throng at the rail. They never slowed their knitting, but their eyes darted back and forth as they listened intently to the exclamations of the others.

"Well?" Mother's voice was low, but Ruth could hear her impatience.

"Not so many houses as Mackinac, I think." Ruth called up to the boys. "Ned! What do you see?'

"Lots of wigwams on the shore. Lots of canoes. I don't see any soldiers—there's no flag at the fort."

The aunts exchanged glances. So the rumors were true—the garrison had been ordered away. Since Indian relations at Fort Dearborn had been peaceful for some time, the officers at Mackinac suspected the regiment would be withdrawn to Green Bay. Ruth often heard the women debating whether the garrison's

Wigwam
A Native American shelter built with a arched frame of branches covered with sheets of bark or hides.

show of force was the reason for that peacefulness. Would the abandoned fort invite trouble?

The breeze freshened as if to speed them along to their journey's end. Men and boys who climbed aloft for better viewpoints excitedly called down news to the womenfolk on the deck.

"Plenty of good, tall trees!"

"Not so many as New York!"

"Poor excuse for a settlement—and not a proper house in the whole place!"

"Doesn't matter—we're not staying around here long anyhow!"

Suddenly, Loring began waving wildly. "Look! It's my pa and Henry! And Ma! And there's Louisa and Lucy!" Faint whooping floated to the ship from over the water.

Mother and Sally Ann looked up sharply. Mother's eyes met Ruth's, and she gave the slightest nod, as if agreeing to the unspoken question in all their minds. Ruth called up again.

"Ned! Ned! What about Daidí and Henry? Can you see them?"

Ned shook his head, squinting hard across the water. Uncle Jack's crew scurried importantly among the crowd of gawking passengers, hauling up the sails and preparing to drop anchor. The bustle woke baby Eunice from her doze and Sally Ann caught her up before she could wail her protest.

"What are they doing?" Sally Ann asked fretfully,

121

getting to her feet to dance the baby around and sneak a better look at the approaching shore. "Why are they anchoring way out here? We're so far away still!"

Ned threw his sister a pitying look, smug in his double advantage of a better view and superior knowledge. "There's no pier, Sally Ann, and it's too shallow because of the sandbar here. Uncle Joe says we'll have to use the scow to get ashore."

At the mate's command, the chain was released and the anchor rattled noisily into the lake. The settlers shifted expectantly away from the aft rail to give the crew room to launch the scow. Ned watched impatiently, then leaned over and whispered into Allen's ear. Allen whispered to Loring on the other side, who answered back with a grin, and before anyone could stop them, they had all jumped off the port side with a cheery "See you on shore!"

The splashes startled everyone, including Uncle Jack, but he just laughed and returned to the business of safely anchoring his ship. Mother and the aunts had jumped to their feet, but seeing how quickly the boys were covering the distance to shore, they settled themselves once again and picked up their knitting until it should be their turn to be ferried over. Only Mother stayed standing, watching the swimmers.

Still far from shore, they stopped, apparently trying the sandbar. After a moment, two of the boys continued to shore while the other turned back toward the ship. It was Ned who was hauled up, dripping.

"Had to come back for my boots!" he laughed. "It's like quicksand out there. Fairly sucked these shoes right off my feet! Run for my boots, Amos! Mind you don't make a mess of my box!"

While Amos clambered down into the hold and Ned caught his breath, the others peppered him with questions. How far? How deep? How cold? But soon Amos was back, and Ned laced his boots up tightly before jumping back over the rail.

On shore Loring's family surrounded him excitedly. Other people gathered as well, the men and Indians walking down to the water's edge, the women standing outside their cabin doors to keep an eye on the ship's progress. A few Indians pushed canoes off the sand and paddled out to the ship. From around the corner of the fort, a couple of tall men in shirt sleeves ambled out of the shadows, then quickened their pace, hurrying down to the water's edge.

Ned's booming voice drifted back over the waves as he found firm footing on the sandbar and waded in, sloshing and hollering. Mindless of her dignity, Ruth scrambled up the stack of wagons as nimbly as Ned himself. Mother bit off her instinctive rebuke, and hushed Cordelia's cries of "Me, too!"

"Well?" Mother said urgently. "Well?"

"It's Daidi! Yes! And Henry! They made it before we did!"

123

Mother settled back on the hatch ledge with her knitting. Sally Ann stopped dancing the baby and sat down beside her. Both were smiling quietly, but that wasn't enough for Ruth. She pulled off her bonnet and waved it over her head. By that time Ned had made it to shore, with Daidí and Henry to meet him. They all waved back at her.

Some of the women and children were being lowered into canoes while the crew loaded the scow. It would be a while yet before their turn came. Ruth helped Mariah up on the wagon, and then, in a particularly generous mood, pulled Cordelia up as well.

From their perch they could see Fort Dearborn and the few cabins and wigwams that surrounded it. Far behind the fort was the horizon, with hardly a tree to break the long sweep of prairie. Somewhere out there was their new home.

But their home for the past weeks was quickly being disassembled. Boxes and trunks were hoisted overboard into the waiting scow. The plows and sawmill gears were unbound. Soon they would start unstacking the wagons.

As the deck cleared of cargo and passengers, the ship began to look forlorn and naked, such as Ruth had never seen her. Mariah heaved a dramatic sigh. "And so it's back to cooking and spinning and washing! We will never again adventure together on the high seas!"

"It's a lake not a sea." Ruth pointed out sharply. A swell of confused emotions left her no patience for

Mariah's theatricals. "And when the waves were high, I recollect none of us much like the adventure!" Still, she couldn't help echoing Mariah's sigh. "I thought I couldn't wait to get out of that smelly women's cabin. And yet, now that we're finally here..." Ruth fell silent, layering the sights and sounds and smells in her memory as if she were pressing flowers into a book.

Mama was rolling up her knitting. "It's time, girls." Mariah's mother and baby Susan were already being helped into a canoe, the little girls waiting to join her. Ruth and Mariah climbed off the wagons and gathered their workbags. When it was Ruth's turn to be lowered into a canoe, sudden tears surprised her. As a farmer's daughter and someday a farmer's wife, she would probably never sail on a ship again. She gave a last wild look around and caught Uncle Joe's eye. Something in his smile seemed to understand.

"See you on shore!" he called, and Ruth remembered that this was his last voyage, too. Now that they had arrived at Fort Dearborn, he must relinquish ownership of the *Telegraph*. Captain Naper was now Farmer Naper. Ruth smiled back bravely, and let herself be lowered into the bobbing canoe.

CHAPTER 11

LIFE IN FORT DEARBORN

R uth gripped the sides of the canoe with white fingers as it rode the waves towards shore. She fixed her eyes on the happy reunion of Henry and Sally Ann, whose pretty face absolutely glowed with the delight of being once again with her husband. Soon, very soon now, the canoe would beach and Daidí would be there with his special smile for her.

The scow arrived at the same time, with Gran wedged in between some crates. All the nearby men formed a line to unload the scow. The barrels and crates passed quickly from man to man across the sand to be stacked high on shore, away from the waves. Ruth carefully made her way out of the tipsy canoe and helped Cordelia and Amos out as well. Immediately, Amos and Cordelia ran across the sand and wrapped themselves around Daidí's legs. Ruth wished she was young enough to do the same, but instead she followed sedately, pretending to wait patiently for her chance to greet Daidí.

Noisy and excited, the children broke into each other's stories trying to relate all the adventures of the past weeks at once. Over their heads, Mother and Daidí

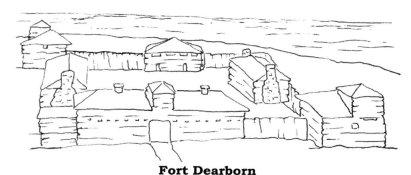

Fort Dearborn
Built on the shore of Lake Michigan in 1803,
occupied on and off for the next thirty years by the military.

carried on a quieter conversation that, from Ruth's observation, consisted mainly of a few simple questions and private, wordless smiles. Ruth kicked at the sand irritably. When would he notice she was standing there? Hadn't he missed her at all?

At last Daidí put the clinging Cordelia to one side so he could step forward. "But I have not yet welcomed my Ruth Eliza! Patiently waiting her turn as always while the rest of us flap and jabber like a flock of blue jays!" Daidí threw his big arms around Ruth, practically lifting her from the ground in a hearty embrace. The well-worn linen of his shirt felt soft on her cheek and smelled of sunshine, tobacco, and horse, just like Daidí always did.

He stood back and took a long look at her, nodding in satisfaction. "It's good to see you again, Cailín!" he said with a warm smile. "I have missed our conversations. Henry is a fine fellow, but he does all the talking! No one else listens to my stories like my wee Cailín." Ruth smiled back, relieved and happy. They might sit on a different fence now or in front of a different fireplace, but she and Daidí would talk together just like the old days in Ashtabula.

As the crew continued to unload the *Telegraph*, the men on shore needed to find storage for the growing pile of crates and barrels and boxes, as well as lodging for their families. The garrison had indeed shipped out only weeks before, so the empty fort provided an excellent place to store and sort the ship's cargo.

Fort Dearborn offered only a few options for travelers. Daidí and Henry had already arranged for lodging at the Eagle Exchange Tavern upriver. Looking down the sandbar, Daidí called out to a small, curly-haired boy of about nine.

"You there! Oliver! Step lively!"

"*Oui, m'sieur?*" the boy panted, running up to them.

"This is Madame Naper and Madame Murray, and these are my children. Will you please guide them to the Eagle Exchange and bring them to Madame your mother?"

"*Oui, m'sieur!* Zees way, *s'il vous plaît!* I haf my canoe here. I weel take you very fast up zee river. I am very strong!" He cocked his head and looked over the group with a practiced eye. "*Mesdames,* you weel like to come first? Ees not very far, but the road, she is very dirty, very wet."

Mother helped Gran into the little canoe while Oliver steadied it. Ruth passed a few bundles to Amos who stood in the water helping hold the boat. While they waited for Oliver to return, Ruth searched for Mariah among the crowd on the beach. With both of them occupied with children and baggage, they barely had time for a quick conversation.

"Mariah! I have to go. We'll be at the Eagle Exchange Tavern. Where are you staying?"

"I don't know—" Mariah consulted quickly with her mother before turning back. "We're at Miller's. It's right across the river from you, I guess. I count on our meeting again soon."

"I'll try. Here comes the canoe—I have to go." Ruth hurried over to where Cordelia waited with the baggage. Oliver ferried them expertly up the river. Before long, it branched out in two directions. Several log taverns already clustered at the fork of the river and more building was under way. They beached the canoe in front of a small cabin marked with a crudely painted blue bird on a weathered board.

"We arrive! Welcome to zee Eagle Exchange Tavern!" Oliver announced.

Ruth scrambled out of the canoe and led Cordelia up the riverbank. Why would Daidí choose this small, shabby tavern? Across the river stood a two-story building, covered in clapboard siding, which Ruth later learned was Mr. Miller's Tavern, where Mariah's family was lodged. A larger dwelling was under construction to abut the little cabin with the blue bird, but at the present, the new building barely boasted the skeleton of a frame.

A round, dark woman backed out of the cabin's door carrying one end of a bench. Mother held the other end. "There you are! Girls, come and meet Madame Beaubien."

As the girls made their curtsies, they heard a sudden clatter, and wailing started up inside the cabin. Two yelping dogs streaked through the doorway, followed by a small boy, but the wailing continued. Madame Beaubien threw up her hands. "*Alors!* What ees now?"

Gran appeared at the door, smiling grimly. "If you have that bench ready, I reckon I'll sit outside for a spell."

Mother settled Gran on the bench, sympathetic and soothing, but when Mother looked up at Ruth, her eyes twinkled with secret laughter. "Take the baggage around back, Ruth. There's a lean-to shed to store it in for now. Then maybe you and Cordelia can help Madame Beaubien by grinding the corn. Her daughter Émilie is back there."

Inside the wailing and scuffling continued, now punctuated by Madame Beaubien scolding in loud, rapid French. Round-eyed, the girls did as they were told, but they longed to see what was going on inside the cabin.

In the shade behind the house, a girl about Cordelia's

age was leaning wearily on her pestle, a knob of wood almost as long as she was tall. A bag full of dried corn sat open against the hollow log in which she had been pounding the grain, and the evidence of her labor was a pathetically small amount of flour in the bottom of a bowl.

While Cordelia and the girl eyed each other, Ruth took charge. "My mother asked me to help you grind corn. With so many more mouths to feed today, I reckon you'll need the help. Let me pound for a while. You and Cordelia can sift it."

A wide grin replaced the girl's sullen expression. She stepped back swiftly for Ruth to take her place and tossed another handful of corn into the trough. Ruth lifted the heavy pestle and let it drop over and over again in rhythm, crushing the dried grains to flour.

Émilie raised her voice to be heard over the noise, delighted to have company in her chores.

Before long, the Murray girls knew the names of all six of Émilie's brothers, when the family had moved to Chicago, and how Émilie longed to be sent to school in Detroit like her cousins who were learning to be genteel ladies. Émilie asked questions of them as well, but rarely waited for an answer. Ruth and Cordelia didn't mind, finding her stories quite interesting and her accent charming.

During a lull in the pounding, Ruth noticed that the wailing had stopped, and Madame Beaubien no longer sounded angry. Even so, Madame Beaubien still chattered excitedly in jumbled French and English and banged pots on her hearth while the children and dogs squabbled. Mother occasionally replied in a low voice, as was her habit. Apparently at the Eagle Exchange Tavern, noise and bustle was their habit!

Ruth's arms and shoulders began to ache from lifting the pestle when a small boy ran around the corner of the cabin bawling for Émilie to bring the flour right away. Cordelia

Mortar and Pestle
A sturdy bowl fitted with a bat-like stick for grinding. Handheld ones grind spices or medicine, bigger ones grind grain and could be made of hollowed-out logs.

finished sifting out the coarser chunks, and Émilie took the bowl to her mamma. The coarse leftovers would be boiled later as hominy, but the cornmeal was needed for today's dinner.

Canoes glided down the river, pulling up in front of the various log taverns scattered along the banks of the fork as grumbling stomachs called the menfolk home. Mariah waved from across the water where she waited for her father and Allen, and Ruth could see Daidí paddling with Ned and a man sporting a shock of wavy hair and wild side-whiskers.

The Beaubien boys drew water for the men to wash and then set up the trestle table under a tree where it was cool and breezy. Cordelia helped cover the table with a cloth that, while much patched, was clean and ironed. She and Émilie set the table with tin plates, knives, and three-tined forks. Glazed earthenware mugs of hard cider stood next to each plate, and a bucket of cool, fresh water stood on a stump nearby with a dipper.

Side Whiskers
Long, bushy sideburns with the beard shaved off from the chin.

Madame Beaubien's French grew shriller and the pot-banging more frenzied. Sent out of the kitchen to take her place as a paying guest, Mother threw Ruth a look. Understanding immediately, Ruth straightened her shoulders and stepped into the hot, noisy darkness of the cabin.

Knowing only a few words of French, Ruth found following Madame Beaubien's frantic directions to be mere guesswork. The hired girl, older than Émilie but still younger than Ruth, fired back at Madame her own unintelligible stream of excuses and retorts. Frying johnnycake was a familiar chore, so Ruth took charge of the spider.

The hearth was roaring hot after a whole morning of preparing food, and Ruth was forced to pull her bonnet over her face to avoid being scorched. Using her apron as a potholder, she pulled the iron skillet close enough to add bacon drippings. When the fat sizzled, she spooned cornmeal mush in dollops around the pan and pushed the pan back onto the hearth. The three legs of the spider suspended the skillet over the glowing coals, and the johnnycakes soon turned brown and crisp.

Ruth turned the cakes, moved them to a wooden platter, and started all over again. Although she still wasn't exactly sure how many people were

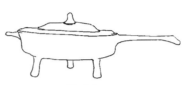

Spider
A frying pan that holds itself up over the coals of a fire on three short legs.

staying at the Eagle Exchange, she figured more than a dozen men, women, and children would be wanting their dinner, and that meant a lot of johnnycake!

The men could be heard unloading the canoe and washing up, which doubled the whirlwind of activity in Madame's kitchen. Two of the little boys were dumped on the bedstead and forbidden to hang so much as a toe off the edge, while the baby, already tied by leading strings to his walking chair, was wedged behind the butter churn so he couldn't scuttle into the way.

Finally Madame surveyed the pots and platters laid out ready on the table and nodded with satisfaction. She washed her face and hands in the bucket by the fire, smoothed back her hair, and changed her apron. With the girls following behind bearing food, Madame

Beaubien sailed out to welcome the guests to her table.

While waiting her turn for dinner had become Ruth's onboard habit, never had the wait been so difficult. Who looked forward to ship's biscuit? But the aromas of

Leading Strings
Strips of cloth attached to a baby's clothes to help hold him upright while he learned to walk.

Madame's bean cassoulet, her baked fish, and the johnnycakes fried in drippings promised a feast.

Unfortunately Monsieur Beaubien's greatest skill was his hospitality. He often called for the hired girl to pour more cider for his guests while he related another story. Spoken in heavily accented English and embellished with outrageous oaths, Monsieur Beaubien's tales had Daidí, Ned and Henry slapping their thighs and roaring with laughter. Ruth even caught Mother smiling, although Mother talked mainly to Sally Ann and pretended not to be listening.

At last Madame called for the dishpan, and she cleaned the plates and utensils while the others had a last draught of water or cider. The men ambled down to the river and paddled back to the fort while the women sat against the shady side of the cabin for a quiet chat. Sally and Madame Beaubien fed their babies, and Gran soon slipped into her afternoon doze.

The children eagerly took their places at the table. Ruth was not disappointed. In spite of the chaos in the kitchen, Madame's cookery tasted even better than it smelled. Now Ruth wished she had helped inside the cabin instead of grinding corn in the shade. Maybe she would have learned Madame's cooking secrets!

Walking Chair
A low box frame or enclosed chair to hold up a baby who couldn't stand or walk alone yet.

In the evening, Daidí and Henry returned with Monsieur Beaubien, their host. Madame had laid out a cold supper of midday's leftovers, a meat pie and some pickled vegetables. The trestle table was drawn out from the trees to take advantage of the setting sun, and the adults dawdled and talked and laughed. Toward the end of the meal, Monsieur Beaubien sent a boy to fetch his fiddle.

Ruth had eaten earlier when helping feed the younger ones. Now tending baby Eunice so Sally Ann could eat, Ruth walked back and forth in the dimness under the trees, highly amused by supper's lively conversation. When Monsieur Beaubien started playing a spirited jig, Daidí's fingers tapped on the table in accompaniment. The mystery of their hotel choice was solved; Daidí was ever attracted to fellow musicians.

Men from the neighboring cabins and log taverns drifted in from the shadows, drawn by the music. As the singing and laughing grew more boisterous, the women excused themselves from the table and headed up to the Beaubien's cabin. Ruth followed, but she would have liked to stay and listen to the music.

The last of supper was tidied away and the children were given a hasty wash from the water bucket. The Eagle Exchange Tavern boasted two pole beds built into the corners, each with a trundle tucked behind its single leg. The ceiling was too low for a loft, so the older Beaubien boys and Amos bedded down on the floor under the table while Cordelia, Émilie, and the little boys snuggled down sideways in the trundle from Madame's bed. Mother and Gran were assigned the other bed with Ruth and Sally Ann sharing the trundle from beneath. A make shift canvas roof had been hastily erected over a section of the unfinished building next door where the men would sleep.

Pole Bed

A bed frame built into the corner of a cabin. Three of its four corners were supported by the walls, so it only needed one leg, or pole, on the fourth corner.

At first Ruth relished the luxury of a real bed, shared with only Sally Ann and the baby. So much more comfort and space than on board the *Telegraph*! But then the mosquitoes started whining around her head. With all difficulties of ship life, at least there were no mosquitoes! Still, it was pleasant to hear the frogs peeping, and the fiddle playing, and occasionally Daidi's voice singing along. It sounded like home.

The next morning when Ruth awoke Madame was already in a bustle. Ruth rolled out of the trundle bed, though it was barely light. Soon enough, coffee boiled on the hearth as well as cornmeal mush, and the hired girl was laying out whatever supper leftovers remained. The boys hauled water and wood, while the girls dressed the children and straightened the cabin. After a hasty breakfast, the men and boys headed back to the fort and Madame started preparing dinner at the cabin. Sally Ann and Gran stayed to help Madame Beaubien, but Mother asked Ruth to go with her to the fort.

Oliver paddled Mother and Ruth down the river, landing the canoe on one of the sandy banks at the mouth. Several of the *Telegraph*'s families were staying at the fort, but those who took lodgings in taverns, like the Murrays, sent someone along to look after their interests. Preparations for the overland crossing were under way.

The very last of the cargo and equipment had been unloaded from the *Telegraph*. Now the provisions needed sorting and the wagons reassembling before packing up could begin. Mother and Ruth, like women from the other families, came to check on their household goods, unpack their kitchen equipment, and ready themselves for this next part of the journey.

While Ruth, with Ned's help, dragged the family's gear into one corner of the fort, Mariah arrived with her mother and Allen. Much too busy to stop, Ruth could only catch Mariah's eye and smile, but Ruth trusted they would find a moment to talk during the morning.

Adding to the activity were sailors loading pelts, honey, and salted pork from the fort's storerooms onto the *Telegraph*. Indians and settlers, interested in looking at the newcomers and the things they had brought from the east, milled about as well. As only the second ship to drop anchor in Chicago that year, the *Telegraph*'s arrival was treated like a holiday.

During the morning, Ruth and her father checked the sacks of cornmeal for bugs and dampness. As he worked, Daidí hummed under his breath. When Ruth caught a few notes, she recognized it as a hymn that they often sang back in Ashtabula.

"It seems odd, Daidí," Ruth said suddenly, "that it's the Sabbath today, and yet there's no meeting in this town, not even a hymn-singing."

"Fort Dearborn is still a frontier settlement, Cailín. There's too much work to do to take time for hymn-singing. And Illinois has wide boundaries and few people. I don't suppose they even get circuit riders way out here."

A man working nearby rose to his town's defense. "Why sir, that ain't true at all! We had a preacher just last month—Elder Beggs. He preached at us twice, sir, and I reckon that'll last us for a while."

Daidí gravely begged the man's pardon, but Ruth could see laughter in his eyes.

The long morning felt unreal, as if Ruth were awake in her own dream. Working so busily after weeks of boredom on the ship, she expected the time to fly by. But the sun only inched across the sky, and though the lake breeze was refreshing, it couldn't blow away the eerie feeling. While she worked, she thought about Ashtabula, remembering it as if it were the story of some other girl's life.

The strange atmosphere infected all of the *Telegraph*'s party, who performed their tasks nearly silently, almost cringing at the loud voices of the locals. When the dinner hour finally arrived, people scattered to their lodgings, eating quickly and without pleasure, and returning as soon as possible.

Glancing around, Ruth realized every one of the *Telegraph*'s passengers had returned to the lakefront, including the youngsters and Granny Naper. As a body, they drifted down to the sandbar where the scow was beached. Mr. Smith, the first mate, stood near the boat talking with Uncle Jack and Uncle Joe.

"Already?" Ruth thought wildly. "They're leaving already?" She clutched at Mother's sleeve. With Gran leaning heavily on her arm, Mother couldn't do more than give Ruth a reassuring smile as they made their way across the sand.

Farewells were said, accompanied by fervent handclasps, a few embraces, and brave tears from Aunt Betsy. Ruth's little cousins Georgie and Jay played in the sand, almost too absorbed to kiss their father good-bye. Ruth watched Uncle Jack clap Ned on the back and pump Daidi's hand, but the scene still had a dreamlike haze. The men climbed into the scow and pushed off toward the *Telegraph*, waiting at anchor in deeper water.

As the length of water widened between the boat and the beach, the eyes of the two brothers met. From the scow, Captain Jack raised his hand in a final salute to Farmer Joe on land, who nodded back, solemnly and firmly. Now Georgie and Jay first realized that their father had left without them and started to wail. Aunt Almeda put her arm around Aunt Betsy as they watched the scow hauled aboard.

The crew moved about on the ship, hauling in the anchor, and unfurling the sails. Immediately catching a stiff breeze, the white canvas swelled with a suddenness that drew a sigh from onlookers back on shore. Proudly, serenely, the *Telegraph* skimmed along the blue water of Lake Michigan.

Still glancing over their shoulders, people began moving back to the fort. While the ship was a beautiful sight, the settlers couldn't spare time to watch with so much work yet to do. Mother and Gran started up the beach, and Ruth joined them. Aunt Betsy and Aunt Almeda walked very slowly, children frisking around their skirts like a litter of puppies. Only Uncle Joe stayed on the beach until the tiny speck that was the *Telegraph* disappeared on the horizon.

CHAPTER 12

JOURNEY ON THE PRAIRIE

When Ruth walked up to the fort with Mother the next morning, Mariah ran out to meet her. "Did you hear the news?" Mariah called out excitedly before Ruth was halfway there.

"What news?"

"About Mrs. Boardman. She had her baby last night. It's a boy!" Mariah fell in step with them, panting a little.

"And Mrs. Boardman?" Mother asked.

"She's feeling fine. All the ladies are saying she had an easy time of it. The fort's surgeon—he stayed when the garrison went to Green Bay—he came to see her, but they sent him away."

Mother turned to Ruth. "I'm going to stop in and pay my respects. Would you please get started on repacking the cornmeal until I get back?"

Ruth and Mariah snatched a few more moments to discuss the news before setting to work. The Boardman girls apparently were delighted with the new baby, and even their brother Horace seemed pleased. Mrs. Boardman had declared in her blunt way that the baby's birth couldn't have happened at a more inconvenient time and that she was eager to get back to packing. Yet she remained on her bed cradling little Charles. Mariah said it was whispered that Mrs. Boardman was especially anxious for this little one's health. Sabra, who was nearly six now, was the last baby who lived.

Covered Wagon
Large wagon fitted with bent wood arches and a fabric cover for some protection from the weather. With steel-rimmed wooden wheels, no steering and no shock absorbers, only cargo and those unable to walk actually rode in them.

The wagons were ready for packing, the wheels reattached and well greased, and the linen bonnets drawn tightly over the bows. Not every family was continuing to the DuPage River site, however. In accordance with their agreement, Mr. Peck and Uncle Joe split their cargo of calico, rum, and other trade goods so that each might set up a trading post. Uncle Joe would trade out of the river settlement, while Mr. Peck did business in Chicago. Every house and cabin was nearly bursting at the seams now, but Mr. Peck was in negotiations with a brother of Monsieur Beaubien's to rent space until he could build something new.

The Bond brothers decided to stay in Fort Dearborn, and the Graves family as well. Traveling the road from Detroit convinced Mr. Graves that traffic would only increase and he was eager to build himself another tavern. While the Chicago settlement couldn't compare to the gracious society of Detroit, Louisa much preferred it to the isolation of a homestead. She was content to run her father's hotel if it meant she could remain where unmarried men outnumbered available girls more than two to one.

After another day or two, Daidí and Henry brought the oxen, horses, and cattle from the far meadow and penned them near the fort. Early tomorrow morning, the men would hitch the wagons and start for the DuPage River settlement.

Ruth stood behind the Eagle Exchange and looked out over the prairie. It stretched to the horizon, flat and green, with only occasional tufts of trees breaking the sweep of grass. The last barrel and bundle had been stowed in their wagon. Soon she would have a hasty supper of Madame's cold meat pie before climbing into the trundle with Sally Ann. This was

Ox

A large cow-like animal, stronger than a horse, used to pull wagons.

the last night she'd sleep in a real bed for weeks, maybe even months. Until the Murrays built their cabin, a blanket on the ground would be her bed. And even once they had a home, she'd be lucky to have a pallet on the floor stuffed with dried grass.

Still, Ruth was too excited to sleep. She watched the

145

sky turn red, wondering what their new home would look like and whether they would be happy there. She already missed the trees and valleys of Ashtabula. Uncle Joe laughingly admitted he couldn't produce valleys, but assured her she would find trees clustered around the little river.

"Think how easy it will be to haul water!" he teased. "And no hills to climb when you go calling on your neighbors. Yes, it's different, but you'll grow fond of it, Ruth. We'll all grow fond of it."

Deep blue crept across the sky, chasing the red sunset. Ruth gave a little sigh, and turned back to the cabin to have her supper and try to sleep.

For all the excitement and bustle leaving Fort Dearborn in the cool of the morning, Ruth ate her dinner still in site of the fort. Lying so low near the lake, the Chicago settlement was built on wet and swampy land. As Oliver warned, the dirt roads were muddy and rutted and wet weather all spring certainly had not improved them. The oxen strained to pull the fully loaded wagons, and just past the boundaries of Chicago, the marsh grew worse before it grew better.

The wheels were mired in mud and water up to their hubs. Each wagon had a team of two oxen, sufficient for most travel, but not enough to drag a wagon through such a swamp. Daidí and the other men left some of the wagons sitting behind on higher ground and walked their oxen teams into the marsh, hitching them to the lead rig.

Six teams were needed to yank the wagon out of the mud with a sucking, squelching sound. Once they led the oxen far enough away to a dry trail, they unhitched them and drove them back to pull the next wagon through.

Mrs. Boardman started the crossing on her wagon's board seat, but the constant danger of pitching out with her baby forced her to retreat to the wagon bed. Even back there, the jolting caused such discomfort and the threat of shifting boxes such concern, that she climbed down and walked. Trying to hold up her long skirts as well as the child proved too much for her strength, however, and Captain Boardman took the infant from her until she regained solid footing.

Seeing Mrs. Boardman's experience, Daidí and Uncle Joe thought it best that Gran cross on horseback. Refusing to sit astride, as true ladies never rode like men, Granny Naper perched regally on top of her horse while Uncle Joe led her through the marsh. Only when Ruth walked close enough did she notice Gran's gnarled fingers were white from clutching the horse's mane.

Fording the marsh with all the wagons lasted until the sun passed its high point. Stopping for a late dinner, the settlers gathered under the meager shade of a clump of ash trees. The men particularly were plastered with stinking black mud from their struggles of the morning, but everyone wore some mark from their trip through the swamp.

Extra johnnycakes and slabs of ham fried up

yesterday at their lodgings provided a satisfying cold lunch. While they rested in the shade and let their clothes dry, Ruth noticed that every adult sat with their backs to Lake Michigan, looking instead out across the prairie.

Ruth and Mariah ate together, taking advantage of the first real chance to talk privately since leaving the *Telegraph*. When Uncle Joe rallied the group to move on, they continued as they walked.

"We've hardly had a chance to do more than say hello! Pa wouldn't allow me to take the ferry over the river, and we were all so busy at the fort. Is Mrs. Beaubien as cross-tempered as they say? And tell me about Mr. Beaubien—Mrs. Miller says he swears like a trapper. She won't let her son go near him any longer 'cause he's learned some dreadful oaths in French!"

Ruth laughed. "Well, I wouldn't take Monsieur Beaubien as a model for a little boy either! Mother went quite red several times! Fortunately, his accent is so thick I mostly couldn't understand what he was saying! But he can play every song you ever heard on the fiddle. And Daidí never could resist good music!"

Ruth went on to tell of Madame's cassoulets and meat pies. Mariah sighed. Mrs. Miller's dinners, while plentiful, seemed more foreign than Madame's. Raised in the South, by a mother who was herself reared by Indians, Mrs. Miller's cooking style did not suit Mariah's taste. Still, the story of the abduction and rescue of Mrs.

Miller's mother almost made up for the disappointing dinners, and a couple hours sped away as they talked it over.

The train of wagons followed an Indian trail mainly traveled by foot or occasionally ponies. The wagons moved with difficulty down the narrow path worn into the prairie. Grasses waist-high, and sometimes higher, flanked

Prairie
Grasslands, mainly flat or gently rolling, with few trees.

them on either side, and the rutted road rocked and bounced the laden rigs.

Granny Naper, the new mothers and the youngest children rode in the wagons, but nearly everyone else walked. The oxen moved slowly, so Ruth and Mariah were able to stay in front of the wagons and out of the dust churned up by their wheels. Uncle Joe, Daidí, and a few other men rode ahead on horseback, scouting and securing the trail.

Away from the lake breezes and with no trees to shelter them, the late afternoon sun scorched the shoulders of Ruth's dress and the top of her bonnet. She pulled the brim low to protect her fair skin, which prevented any breath of air from cooling the sweat prickling on her forehead.

"My feet hurt!" Cordelia whined, lagging behind.

"Mine, too, but we have to keep going." Ruth took Cordelia's hand to drag her along. "I heard the guides from the fort say we're pushing on a little farther, and then we'll stop for the night. There's a creek up ahead. We'll have fresh water. And grass for the cattle. Just a little bit farther."

With their heads down to keep the sun out of their eyes, and the noise of the lumbering wagons drowning all other sounds, the girls didn't see the outrider until he was almost upon them.

It was Uncle Joe on his horse, Old Bill. "Not too much farther!" He called with an encouraging smile. "We found the creek and you're nearly there!"

A clearing of beaten down prairie grass served as a campsite. But a host of chores needed to be worked through before they could rest. The oxen pulled the wagons around the clearing before the men and boys unhitched them and led them down to the creek to drink. Women and girls unloaded cooking and sleeping gear while the children gathered firewood.

Amos and Cordelia toted water from the creek back to the campsite, which lay just outside of the cool shade of the trees. "Why do we have to be so far away from the creek?" Cordelia complained. "It's so much nicer under the trees, and we wouldn't have to carry the buckets so far!"

"You'll be thankful later, Cordelia," Ruth assured her. "Once the sun starts to set, the mosquitoes will be out and hungry. Here in the open, we'll have a better chance of a breeze to blow them away."

The outriders had started a fire with their flint and steel as soon as they chose the campsite. Each family fetched a few coals in a pot to light their own cooking fires. Soon the smell of sizzling pork and boiling coffee drifted across the prairie. Before they left the Beaubiens, Mother had filled a pottery crock with cracked corn and water to soak while they traveled. Now Ruth scooped out the lumpy porridge to cook in the frying pan, and refilled the crock with beans and water for tomorrow. By the time Daidí and Ned returned from hobbling the animals for the night, the salt pork and hominy stew was thick and bubbling hot.

Twilight fell while Mother prepared some dried meat in the dutch oven and nestled it in the coals to simmer overnight. Ruth took Amos and Cordelia down to the creek to splash off some of the swamp mud and sweat-encrusted dust. She also dabbled her own sore and dirty feet in the water. Weeks of living on the ship had

Dutch Oven
Iron lidded pot that baked food like an oven when buried in coals.

151

softened them and she was unused to the rocks and sharp-edged grasses.

Finally Ruth crawled under the wagon box with her blanket and lay down beside her brothers and sister. The mosquitoes never bothered her, whether the hoped-for breeze blew up or not, for she instantly fell into a deep sleep.

Daidi climbing out of the wagon woke Ruth while the sky was barely gray. He called in a low voice to Ned, who grunted and sighed and finally unrolled himself from his blanket. Over her head, Ruth heard Mother moving around in the wagon, tossing her quilt over the bonnet to air and unpacking breakfast needs.

Subdued noises rose from each family's camp and a few birds chirped in anticipation of sunrise, but a sleepy stillness yet prevailed. Ruth climbed out from under the wagon with her blanket. While the dewy grass cooled her bare feet, the quilt felt cozy wrapped around her shoulders as she stood there in the early half-light, listening.

Quiet rarely happened, Ruth suddenly realized. All day long the wagons creaked and jangled. Dozens of feet— oxen, horses, cows, people—tramped on the hard road. When the wagons stopped, dishes clattered and children cried as people went about their chores. Even as she dropped off to sleep the night before, the last thing Ruth remembered was the deafening shrill of tree frogs and insects.

Back home in Ashtabula, Ruth would squeeze her eyes shut and pretend to be sleeping until she heard Mother call. By that time, she knew the fireplace would again be dancing with flames and Daidí would be pulling on his boots, talking to Mother as she started breakfast. Only then would Ruth rise, joining the comfortable bustle and noise. Once or twice when she was ill, Ruth had awakened early. The dark silence felt so eerie and empty that she huddled under her blankets, afraid to move until the familiar morning sounds finally began again.

On this morning, however, the quiet felt like a special treat, a privilege only allowed to those who appreciated it. Once Amos and Cordelia woke, the camp would be alive with activity. The spell would be broken.

Mother swung her leg over the side of the wagon, carefully holding back her skirts to find a foothold on a wheel spoke. She stood beside Ruth without speaking, sharing the moment. Then she reached out and smoothed back the sandy wisps of Ruth's tousled hair.

"Time to get breakfast, Ruth Eliza."

The enchanted pause melted like snow on the hearth. The real day began.

Ruth slipped her dress on over her chemise and tied up the front, giving Cordelia and Amos a nudge with her foot while she did so. "Wake up, slug-a-beds! We can't

Chemise

A long shirt worn to bed as a nightgown or under a dress as a slip.

153

make breakfast without water and wood."

Mother pulled the iron pot from the coals of yesterday's fire. The dried meat, now plump and tender, sent a savory smell across the campsite. The younger Murrays sniffed appreciatively, scattering to collect firewood and draw water. Soon the big cauldron boiled furiously on the hot fire and Ruth started preparing the cornmeal mush.

Boiling mush required constant stirring or it would cook lumpy, or worse yet burn on the bottom. Few foods tasted as disgusting as burnt mush, but with no food to spare, it would have to be choked down anyway, souring the stomachs and the moods of the whole family. While Ruth attended the fire, Cordelia and Amos shook out and folded the blankets, refilled the water barrels, and helped Mother pack up the wagon.

Daidi and Ned returned from seeing to the cattle just as the sun peeked over the far prairie horizon. Tin plates of hot mush and stew disappeared quickly, half carefully put away for midday. The freshly watered oxen were hitched up to the wagon, stomping and blowing, and as soon as Uncle Joe gave the signal, Ned flicked his long switch over the animals' heads and called, "Come up!" The big beasts lurched forward, the wheels rolled, and the wagon

Gooseberry
A shiny green berry, a little tart when eaten raw.

took its place in line. Mother, Ruth, and the children followed behind.

Early morning clothed the prairie in its softest, most flattering colors. The long grasses looked green and fresh and billowed in endless waves on either side of the trail.

Flowers of purple and yellow glowed in the pink light. No dust swirled behind the wagons yet as the track was still moist with dew, and the coolness made walking pleasant.

Ruth found Mariah and they picked wildflowers as they walked, braiding the flowers' long stems into crowns for the little ones. They even made a couple of wreaths to slip on the great horns of Buck and Dandy, Mr. Sisson's oxen. Buck rolled his eyes, but allowed the giggling girls to adorn him without breaking his measured pace.

Wildflowers

Flowers that bloomed on the sunny prairie including sunflowers, asters, purple coneflowers and black-eyed susans.

Late in the morning, Mother called to Ruth and Cordelia. "Here, girls. Take this sack and run up ahead. I believe those are gooseberry bushes on that rise."

"Gooseberries! Mmm!" Cordelia said, jumping up and down.

"Take Mariah and her sisters with you. I'm sure there's plenty for everyone. But pick fast or we'll leave you behind!" The girls dodged around the other wagons, eager for the treat.

Because of the cool spring, many berries were still unripe, but the branches hung low with an abundance of fruit. Soon nearly all of the children flitted through the bushes like a flock of cardinals, hurrying to pluck the shiny berries before the line of wagons passed. As the dust from the last wagon settled, the children gathered themselves together and flew past the plodding oxen to light on a new berry patch up ahead.

Just before midday, a stand of trees rose up on the horizon, signaling a possible creek and a pleasant stopping place for dinner. The oxen and horses, as well as the settlers, enjoyed a long, cool drink of water. Families grouped together to eat, chat, or maybe even nap. Mother shared out the meat and mush left from breakfast, now cold and stiff in the pot. Ruth took her slab and a handful of gooseberries and sat with Mariah on a mossy rock overlooking the creek.

"Feels like we've been traveling all our lives, doesn't it?" Ruth said thoughtfully. "Always going somewhere, somewhere we don't even know. And we won't ever go home again when the traveling is over. In just a couple days, Uncle Joe will tell us we're home, but it won't be like home at all."

Mariah tossed a pebble into the water and watched the

ripples spread out in wide circles with her head tipped to one side. Pretend stories tumbled from her lips without effort, but expressing her real thoughts came less easily. Finally she turned to Ruth, her pretty face puckered with concentration.

"But it is home. You have your ma and pa, and your brothers and sisters. Even your granny. And wherever the lot of you make your beds, that is your home."

"Oh, I know I'm lucky to be with my family, but still—"

"No! It's more than that. It's, it's—" Mariah took a deep breath and tried again. "When Ella was born we lived in Indiana. I helped wash her baby linen and hung it on the witch hazel bushes to dry. Cassie was born in New York, and I hung her linen over the fence in back. Now here's little Susan, and I hang her cloths in the wagon so they dry while we travel. No matter where we go, there's always a baby, always our chores, always Pa planting in the spring and smoking pork in the fall. It always feels like home."

The two girls sat quietly. Maybe Mariah was right and home wasn't the place you live, but the people you live with. But the people you live with change, too, Ruth thought. Now Gran and Aunt Betsy lived with them, while Sally Ann no longer did. And people change within themselves as well. When Sally Ann married, Ruth stepped up to the new role of oldest daughter at home. "At home" hadn't changed, but she had.

Ruth wasn't sorry when Uncle Joe called for the

wagons to move on. The puzzle could wait until they arrived at their new "home." She'd think about it then. Maybe she could ask Daidí about it some night as they sat over the remains of a fire.

CHAPTER 13

CALLING ON MRS. LAWTON

The afternoon's journey proved less pleasant. Clear skies meant unrelenting sun. The colors of the prairie bleached into a monotonous glare seen through the dust hanging in the air. Sweating and gritty, Ruth wondered again what the lure of the prairie was. What she wouldn't give for some trees right now!

As the afternoon waned, Uncle Joe dismounted, walking alongside the wagons and talking with each family. Ruth caught glimpses of him up ahead when the trail dipped and rose as he worked his way back through the line. Not much longer until he reached them.

Uncle Joe fell in step to talk with Ned, who was driving the oxen. Mother joined them, and Ruth drew nearer as well. "What's the news, Joe?" Mother asked. "It's getting late."

"Yes, but there's no place to stop. The guides say that if we push on a little farther, we can make the Aux Plaine River yet today."

"How much farther?"

"Well, that's hard to say. We're moving a little slower than I'd hoped. Before sundown, certainly. That is the

159

best place to cross the river with wagons, and a couple of men run a trading post and tavern nearby."

Mother looked up with interest. "A trading post and tavern?"

"I knew that would get your attention!" Uncle Joe laughed. "I believe they both have wives and families with them as well. You can hear what prairie life is like first hand."

The promise of a little socializing reenergized the company. The little ones made it a game to look ahead through the dust clouds for signs that the river was near. Before long, a tree line appeared on the horizon. The menfolk cussed at and encouraged their cattle while the females smoothed back their hair under their bonnets.

The Aux Plaine doubled back on itself here in a crooked dogleg, slowing the river and widening it until it was shallow enough for wagons to cross fairly safely. Usually by summer the water barely trickled through the rocks, forcing voyageurs on their way to the big river to carry their canoes overland until past the turn. This year's rains still rushed down the riverbed, a boon to the voyageurs, but an added danger to wagons crossing the ford.

Two brothers named Lawton had settled along the river, building a series of rough cabins that served as farmhouse, trading post, and tavern. After consulting with the guides from Fort Dearborn, the Lawtons walked out to meet the wagon train and direct the travelers to a

160

CALLING ON MRS. LAWTON

Voyageurs
The men who worked for the fur companies hunting, trapping and carting supplies. They often traveled by canoe.

suitable campsite for the night. With evening fast approaching, fording the river would wait until tomorrow.

Socializing would have to wait as well. First the men needed to water and hobble the animals while the women prepared supper. Everyone knew their chores and scattered purposefully, the promise of paying a call at the Lawton's later spurring them on.

Cordelia scouted for firewood while Ruth laid the fire and fetched a coal to start it. By using the driest wood and some careful blowing, Ruth soon had a good fire blazing. Mother prepared a prairie chicken, one of several brought down by the outriders earlier in the day. After weeks of bacon, the variety was greatly anticipated, and there were enough prairie chickens for every family to have a taste.

Ruth set the spider in the fire and started melting lard in it. Mother added pieces of the prairie chicken along with some wild onion, and the delicious smell made

Ruth's mouth water. The cornmeal mush she stirred on the other side of the fire didn't provoke the same reaction, yet Ruth knew it was the mush that would keep her belly from pinching in hunger.

Prairie Chicken
A speckled wild bird weighing less than two pounds.

As the chicken stewed, Ruth and Cordelia alternated stirring with unpacking the wagon. Mother walked down to the river to wash the dust from her face in anticipation of meeting the Lawton families. When she returned, Daidí and Ned were with her, also freshly washed with their wet hair slicked back from their foreheads.

"Mmm! That sure smells good, Cailín! It was calling to me all the way down river where we were watering the oxen. Made me so hungry, I almost took a bite out of Brighty's ear!"

"Daidí!" Cordelia protested. "Brighty would not like you biting his ear!" The big milky-white ox was her favorite.

"Save me your sermon, little preacher. I reckon I wouldn't like biting his ear either. I'm sure I would much prefer some of that prairie chicken stew. Can you spare a bowlful for your old father, Cailín?" He settled himself on the ground with his back against the kitchen supplies trunk.

Ruth mounded tin plates with steaming mush and carefully ladled a portion of fragrant stew over each mound. Mother took a seat on the trunk by Daidí, but the rest of the family just sat cross-legged around the fire. Conversation was reduced to sighs of contentment as they savored the special treat.

With every dish licked dry, cleaning up after supper was a simple chore. Mother banked the fire and nestled a pot of beans and bacon into the coals to bake overnight. Ruth poured the extra mush she'd made into a greased bowl and covered it with a plate. By morning it would be firm enough to slice and fry in bacon fat, if the raccoons didn't get it. She wedged it carefully under the wagon wheel near her bedroll where she could keep an eye on it.

The other families also tidied their campsites and started to gather. Even the children wanted a good look at the homesteaders before they turned in for the night. Through shadowy twilight the small crowd moved together toward the pale glow in the woods that spilled from the tavern's open door.

The proprietor, Mr. Barney Lawton, came out to welcome them to his establishment. While only a log house, it was twice the size of the Eagle Exchange tavern and boasted two public rooms in addition to the family's quarters. The men crowded around the bar in one room. Mr. Barney cordially invited the women to wait on his wife in the dining room.

Mrs. Lawton welcomed them eagerly. Barely older than

Sally Ann, she had a pinched face with close-set eyes and was all bones and angles except for an enormous belly swollen with her expected child. Lowering herself awkwardly into the only chair, she sent the little servant girl to make tea. The other women squeezed onto the benches that surrounded the table.

Ruth stood behind Mother, listening as the women talked. Or rather, as Mrs. Lawton talked. Recently married, Mrs. Lawton found the prairie lonely. She lit up like a pinecone on a campfire at this chance to air her grievances to a new audience. The other women murmured politely, but it was Mrs. Boardman who firmly turned the conversation by asking pointed questions about the land, the weather and the native population.

While Mrs. Lawton talked, a Potawatomi woman slipped in through the doorway. She was dressed in a combination of Indian and European clothing and was as plump as Mrs. Lawton was skinny. A small boy clung shyly to her skirts.

Mrs. Lawton's eyes flicked over her, although she didn't stop talking. Finally accepting that her guests were preoccupied with the newcomer, she made a rather sulky introduction.

"This is my sister-in-law, Mrs. David Lawton, and her boy Joseph. She doesn't hardly speak English."

Mrs. David's round face remained passive, but her dark eyes glittered, and Ruth guessed she understood much more English than she spoke. "How do you do's" were politely exchanged, along with the usual "What a fine boy," and then the girl brought in tea.

Aunt Almeda once entertained Ruth and Mariah with stories of wealthy families in Buffalo. She told them young ladies were sent to school to achieve a gracious manner and learn how to pour out tea most elegantly. People owned whole tea sets with cups, saucers, teapots, and sugar bowls made of the finest china, so delicate you could see light through it, and painted with the most charming flowers. Four cups on the servant girl's tray looked just like those Aunt Almeda described, but there were also several tin cups and a chipped clay mug.

As Mrs. Lawton poured out the tea, the little servant handed it around, her eyes darting nervously about the room as she tried to assess each guest. Who was the most important woman in the room? Who should receive the china cup and who the chipped mug? Ruth caught an amused smile on Aunt Almeda's lips before it was politely wiped away.

By excluding herself, her sister-in-law and any woman who looked unmarried, Mrs. Lawton managed to serve all her guests at once, a triumph for a hostess in the wilderness. Mrs. Lawton became much more amiable as the conversation continued, but while willing to answer the women's questions about their new home, she, as a new bride, didn't have many answers.

Ruth could tell when Mother and the other women decided Mrs. Lawton's company was no longer preferable to sleep by the slight glances they gave each other. Mrs. Boardman started the farewell rituals, with Aunt Almeda smoothing out her abruptness with more courteous language, and the others made appropriate noises in the background.

Mrs. David Lawton elected to leave at the same time, passing their camp on her way downriver to her cabin at the trading post. Mrs. Sisson, who had lived near a band of Potawatomi in Indiana, conversed with her using a few words she remembered. Although no information of real interest was exchanged, Mrs. David became almost as animated as Mrs. Barney had been. It was simple enough to guess that she was just as lonely as her sister-in-law, and Ruth wondered at the pigheadedness of the two women. Married to brothers and the only souls for miles in the wilderness, yet not friendly to each other.

The men returned to camp quite a bit later. Ruth heard them because she slept lightly, on the look out for raccoons going after the mush. Still, Daidí called to Ned in the morning while it was yet dark and they went down to fetch the cattle. Mother started the fire. Ruth woke Amos and Cordelia. Another day began.

Fording the Aux Plaine was the morning's first task. While running deeper than usual for July, the Aux Plaine was still a shallow river with a solid, rocky bed, and the Lawton brothers assured them there would be no difficulties. Once they struck camp, yoked the oxen, and lined up the wagons, Mr. Barney went across on his horse to show them the best way. The horse seemed to have sure footing in the rushing water and barely even got its belly wet.

Mr. Sisson, having the most experience with wagon-travel, led his team down first. He climbed up to the seat where Allen already waited. Behind him in the wagon, Mrs. Sisson and the girls were wedged in between the barrels and trunks, cushioned with comforters and featherbeds.

"Hang on tight!" he warned Allen, grasping a bow of the bonnet himself. Then he flicked the goad over the oxen's shoulders. "Come up, Dandy! Come up, Buck!" The big animals lunged forward. Although barely sloped, the embankment pushed the wagon a little faster than the oxen would normally pull it, and they found themselves hurried into the water before they knew it. Buck's big eyes rolled nervously a moment, but as the water barely splashed his knees, he settled down right away with Dandy to haul the wagon across.

Goad

A long stick for prodding an animal, used with verbal commands.

While solid enough, holes and bumps in the rocky bottom proved more challenging to the wagon than Mr. Barney's horse. The oxen moved forward placidly, but behind them, the wagon jerked and swayed from side to side as the iron-rimmed wheels felt their way along the rock. Not as long-necked as horses, Dandy and Buck had to hold their great heads high to keep the water out of their noses.

At last the two beasts found dry footing on the far side of the river. Heaving under their yoke, they clambered up the bank, dragging the wagon up with them. Soft sounds behind her made Ruth realize she wasn't the only one holding her breath until the Sissons were safely across.

Another wagon creaked down the embankment and prepared to enter the river. Daidí and Ned switched places, with Ned on horseback and Daidí driving the wagon team. Young Ira Carpenter had been serving as driver of Aunt Betsy's wagon in Uncle Jack's stead, but Daidí figured he or Uncle Joe would come back and take the crossing. Fording a swiftly-moving stream asked for a little more experience than Ira had so far gathered.

When the Murrays' turn arrived, Ruth, Mother and Cordelia wedged themselves into the bottom of the wagon. Since the sideboards were only a little over knee high, a sudden bump could easily throw someone off balance and over the edge.

"Amos!" Mother called sharply. "Come and sit down right now!"

Ruth tucked her skirt around her knees to make room for Amos to squeeze in beside her, but he was still peering out the back. Cordelia had already snuggled up in Mother's lap. Sitting down so low, they couldn't see anything, but they could hear the river splashing against the bottom of the wagon box. As one of the wheels bounced over hidden rocks, something shifted behind Ruth, poking her painfully in the back. Half-standing, she reached behind to try to shove it back.

At that moment, two wheels rolled into a crevice and the wagon rocked sharply to one side. Out of the corner of her eye, Ruth saw Amos pitch over the backboard and she lunged for him without thinking. With the wagon swaying so crazily, she lost her balance and hit the cold water before she knew what was happening.

Spluttering, Ruth surfaced right away and tried to find her footing. She knew the stream wasn't more than waist deep, but the smooth rock bed was slippery with algae and the rushing water caught at her long skirts and dragged her downriver.

A quick glance behind surprised her. The wagon was already a good walk back. But where was Amos? While she wanted desperately to thrust both legs down and try to stand, Daidí had often warned them to keep their feet up for fear they'd catch on a branch or log. Better to stay afloat and head for the shallows, although her heavy skirts made floating difficult.

She glimpsed Amos ahead of her slipping downstream like a fallen leaf. His head was up and he grabbed at branches as they passed, so he looked all right. As long as they stayed free and afloat until the river calmed, Ruth thought, everything will be fine.

Smoke in the sky reminded her that Mr. David Lawton's trading post lay downriver of the ford. Would Mr. David be outside to see them? Wasn't there a second ford? Maybe it would be shallow enough to regain their footing. Questions tumbled around in her head, but the river rushed her by too fast to do more than cast a frantic glance at the log house as she skittered across the slimy rocks and then fell over a low drop off into a deep pool.

At first Ruth panicked when she couldn't feel the bottom, but then she realized the deep pool was a calm bypass on the swift stream. Treading water as best she could, she saw Amos, who could swim a little, making his way to some overhanging roots on the edge. Ruth could not swim. But neither did she want to drown in a pool so small a man could spit across it.

With her legs helplessly entangled in her skirts, Ruth flailed her arms back and forth, managing to inch forward toward land. Amos had pulled himself up onto the tree roots and leaned toward her as far as his short arms would let him. Finally she paddled near enough to grasp his hand, and soon she could also reach the tree. Ruth hauled herself onto the bank and just lay there, exhausted. She moved only once—to untie the bonnet that had washed off her head immediately, but was nearly strangling her with the ribbons still wrapped around her throat.

Shouts and rustling in the woods upriver edged into her consciousness. "C'mon, Amos," Ruth encouraged as she struggled to her feet. "Let's see how much trouble we're in."

Hearing the noise, David Lawton and his wife came running just as Barney Lawton and Mr. Sisson burst through the underbrush. "Did you see them? Are they all right?" Mr. Sisson panted. Before David could answer, Ruth and Amos dragged themselves into the clearing from downriver.

"Here we are, Mr. Sisson. We're fine."

"Ruth! Thank the Lord! And Amos, too! Well, I'll be— What were you two thinking!"

Ruth and Amos stood in Mrs. David's dusty yard, bedraggled and dripping. Both knew from experience there was no proper answer other than an apology. Neither of them planned to fall out and nearly drown, and why an adult would assume they did it on purpose was beyond their reckoning, so they just stayed quiet and tried to look repentant.

By this time, more people had thrashed through the weeds on both banks, calling out and anxiously scanning the river for the two children. Mr. Sisson shouted back at them that all was well. Mrs. David tried to draw them into the cabin and in front of the fire, but Ruth shook her head. She just wanted to get back to the wagon, take whatever scolding they were bound to get, and get away from all the fussing.

They met Daidí on the way back. With the fate of his wife, youngest child, and all their household goods in his

171

hands, Daidí had no choice but to watch his children disappear downstream while he maneuvered the wagon to safety on dry land. Now that he'd finally caught up with them, he stopped short, swaying slightly.

He was hatless, his face white with dread, and a red welt from a low branch stood out sharply on his cheek. His broad chest heaved with ragged breaths from his race through the forest. Without a word, he gathered them up in his arms, wet and muddy as they were.

In a few minutes, they rejoined the others back at the ford. Mother arrived right behind Daidí, so their scolding, shortened and tempered by relief, was all over before the Murrays reached the clearing. Her sodden skirts were uncomfortable to walk in, but Ruth looked forward to getting back on the trail and leaving the whole mortifying scene behind.

Chapter 14

The DuPage River At Last

When all the wagons passed safely over the ford, the travelers bid farewell to Mr. Barney Lawton and set out once again across the prairie. The farther they walked from Fort Dearborn, the more overgrown the trail became. Few homesteaders lived out this way, and the natives had migrated to the bounty of their summertime lands, needing no contact with traders at this time of year.

Chilled at first, and still trembling from her unexpected swim, Ruth walked briskly until her clothes started to dry out in the sun. Mariah didn't bother to keep up as Ruth wasn't in much of a mood for conversation. By midmorning Ruth felt more comfortable, both without and within, and she slowed her pace to rejoin Mariah and the other girls.

The sky was clear and blue again, beautiful during the freshness of the earliest part of the day, but an omen of another scorching afternoon on the treeless landscape. Even though the prairie grasses were almost as tall as the wagons, they offered no shade when the sun was straight overhead. And the stalks grew so densely no

173

breeze was allowed through. The path ran on for miles in the airless, dusty gully worn through the grassy thicket.

"It's so hot! Can you see any trees ahead?" Mariah asked Ruth as they trudged along.

"I can't see anything except the Boardman's wagon and all this giant grass! I feel like we're walking in the bottom of a big, green box."

Just then a wall of the big, green box rustled and Uncle Joe's horse fell into step beside them. "That was a close squeeze!" Uncle Joe exclaimed from the saddle. "I pulled Old Bill over as far as we could, and we still almost got scraped by that wagon!"

"Can you see over the grass from up there on Old Bill, Uncle Joe? It must be about time to stop for dinner."

"Well, that's why I'm making my way down the wagon line. There are no trees ahead as far as the eye can see. So when the guides give the signal, we'll just be stopping right on the track."

Ruth and Mariah exchanged glances. Right on the track! With the noonday sun beating down on them! Ruth thought longingly of the dark leafy forests surrounding Ashtabula.

Uncle Joe guided Old Bill into a shallow recess in the wall of grass to let the girls and their wagon pass. "Bacon won't be the only thing frying up at dinner today," Mariah muttered under her breath.

When the call came to halt, boys watered the oxen with buckets, but the poor animals had no escape from the sun. The people, meanwhile, climbed into or crept under their wagons, seeking a little shade during their meal. Insects droned in the still air, a monotonous, stupefying sound broken only occasionally by an ox or horse shaking away flies.

The beans pulled from this morning's fire had barely cooled all morning. Ruth took her share and went to lean against a wheel in the shade of their wagon. As she ate, Ruth wondered when the dampness of her dress had switched from river water to perspiration. It felt much the same.

She jerked awake when Uncle Joe gave the word to move on, surprised to find she had dozed off and suspecting she wasn't the only one. Calls of "Come up" echoed drowsily up and down the line as the oxen slowly heaved the wagons forward once again.

Ruth put one foot in front of the other, her head down, her bonnet pulled low over her face, watching but not really seeing her dusty toes peep out from under her skirt as they scuffed across the baked earth. Sweat trickled, itching, down the middle of her back. An irritating cloud of no-see-ums hung around her head no matter how many times she swatted at them, and she was too hot to swat at them anyhow. Even Mariah walked without chattering, stifled by the heat.

The barest caress of moving air made Ruth look up. The wagon in front blocked her view a little, but the land ahead seemed to slope down. Flowers and seed heads atop the grasses bobbed like whitecaps on a vast green sea. Best of all, the gentle breeze that set them dancing also stirred the moist tendrils of hair on Ruth's neck, remarkably refreshing.

Late afternoon sun slanted into her eyes making it difficult to see. They had followed the trail nearly due west all day. On the horizon of the prairie sea stood an irregular border of trees and brush, suggesting a stream ran across their path up ahead. Ruth's heart jumped under her faded calico. Uncle Joe told them it might take three days to reach the DuPage River. Could that be their new home up ahead?

Ruth didn't feel quite as tired anymore. She and Mariah discussed the possibility with an animation impossible just moments before, and Ruth didn't even complain when Cordelia reached for her hand to be pulled along.

"How far away do you think your Pa will want to settle?" Ruth asked, knowing Mr. Sisson disliked neighbors too close.

"I hope not too far. At least I hope the house is on the edge of the claim so we can walk over to see each other once in a while. I don't think he'd let me ride."

"Maybe we can canoe like they do on the Chicago River! Well, if we had a canoe." Both girls sighed, picturing a lonely autumn.

Mariah brightened suddenly. "We all need houses. Bound to be lots of cabin-raising until every family's

176

settled. I reckon we'll have all sorts of camping parties until the snow comes!"

Far ahead, they could see the outriders approaching the wooded copse and disappearing within the trees. The oxen plodded on, and the girls watched the ridge eagerly for the riders' return. Finally Uncle Joe emerged alone, and headed up the trail to meet the wagons.

Word filtered back through the line to Ruth and Mariah. Yes, it was the DuPage River! But it was the east branch, not the place Uncle Joe and Uncle Jack chose for their settlement. The west branch was still a few miles off, and as the day was already long, they would make camp here for the night.

Ruth considered whether that disappointed her or not. Part of her wanted to prolong the journey, the pause from her usual chores and ordinary life. And yet, another part of her still hoped to go back to that ordinary life when the journey ended. That she would never return to the only home she had ever known seemed like an odd dream.

In reality, the same old Murray family would soon begin their new life in a new state. They would build a new house with a new chimney that hopefully wouldn't smoke as much as the old one did. And waiting one more night was just one more night.

"I guess I'm not much of a deep thinker," Ruth smiled to herself. "But if I stand around philosophizing like a Boston preacher, the bacon will never get itself fried." She shrugged off her thoughts and set out to fetch a coal for the supper fire.

This stretch of the river flowed wide and shallow over a gravel bottom, difficult to dip a bucket into, let alone a waterwheel for a sawmill. Concerns over whether the west branch would be similar were murmured over each family's supper. Uncle Joe walked from campfire to campfire, assuring them that the west branch ran faster and deeper and would need little digging or damming to be the perfect sawmill site.

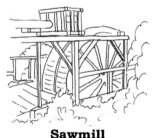

Sawmill

Running water was used to power the machinery that could saw logs into boards.

Leaving Ruth to fry the bacon and johnnycake, Mother took Amos and Cordelia down to the river to wash some of the dust from their necks and faces. Cordelia was still young enough to need the help. Yesterday, Amos would have been sent to clean up on his own, but after today's adventure, Mother and Daidí had clipped his wings. Since Amos was all but tied to Mother's apron strings, Ruth was surprised to see how meekly he submitted to his punishment. The sudden dunk in the Aux Plaines must have cooled some of the rebellion simmering in his eight-year-old breast.

Daidí sat down on the kitchen box and watched Ruth efficiently cooking batch after batch of johnnycake on the iron spider. His hair dripped into his shirt collar, but he looked refreshed after a quick splash while watering the oxen.

"Ruth," he said presently, "your mother told me how it happened this morning. It doesn't surprise me that Amos was too stubborn to sit down like he was told. Nor am I surprised that you tried to save him without thinking of yourself." Bending over the frying pan, Ruth felt her face flush, not entirely from the fire. "This Murray clan would be limping badly if you weren't here for us, Cailín. You have a rare talent."

Ruth looked up, bewildered. "Talent? But I don't sing at all like Sally Ann!"

Daidí chuckled. "Yes, Sally Ann sings like an angel. It's a wonderful gift, but it isn't much use to her while she's learning to run a household. It means a lot to your mother that she can leave the youngsters or the cooking in your hands while she helps Sally Ann and the baby."

He leaned forward with his elbows on his knees, his face suddenly serious. "The way you listen to my old stories—that's also a gift. You know, everyone loves to talk. Not everyone has your talent for listening! When you laugh at my stories, I feel like a fine fellow, as funny as your Uncle Jack. Your gran and your sisters feel it, too. Whether we boast or grumble or talk nonsense, if we can tell it to our Ruth, all is right with the world!"

Daidí sat back on the kitchen box. "I reckon we don't even realize how much we rely on you, but when that river swept you away..." An odd catch in his voice made her look up sharply, but Daidí's eyes crinkled into a grin immediately. "Take a bow, Cailín!" he said heartily, clapping his hands together in enthusiastic applause.

Blushing, Ruth bobbed a little curtsey and bent over the johnnycakes frying in the spider to cover her confusion. People usually applauded singers and storytellers. The gifts Daidí said she had, they seemed so ordinary, so undeserving of applause. Yet Ruth still heard the clapping in her head. She still saw the approval in his eyes.

Mother came back just then with Amos and Cordelia. Ned followed right behind. The Murray family was hungry for supper, and Ruth pushed her puzzling thoughts to the back of her mind.

Ruth's eyes flew open the next morning as soon as Daidí started moving in the wagon box above her head. The sky was still dark, but the birdsong definitely foretold sunrise. Daidí swung himself over the sideboard and helped Mother down, then leaned under the wagon to call to Ned. Ned mumbled and snorted, but Ruth rose eagerly from her last night on the trail. Tonight they would unroll their blankets in the new settlement. Of course it would still feel like camping, but it would be on the site of their new home.

The oxen were hitched up and ready before the gray sky turned pink. Surrounded by trees, Ruth couldn't see the sun peeping over the horizon, but the small clearing brightened enough to finish packing the wagons. Uncle

Joe started off on his horse, and the rest of the group fell in line.

The landscape shifted from tall grass prairie to more frequent thickets of trees, a welcome change for the homesteaders. Most of them hailed from New England's hilly forests and they were used to felling trees and burning stumps before planting. The endless sweep of prairie made them uneasy. If the land didn't produce more than grass, how fertile could it be? These groves of white oaks, good solid hardwood, cheered them considerably.

Ruth, Mariah, and the little girls chattered as they walked the shade-dappled trail, occasionally chasing their own long shadows when they crossed a meadow and had the rising sun at their backs. They gathered sunflowers, asters, black-eyed susans, and blooms Ruth didn't even know the names of, still dewy and sweet-smelling.

As the morning progressed, they entered denser wood just about the time the sun was reaching its height, with the midday break still an hour or two away. Shrubs and weeds tangled in the underbrush, but with the trees towering high overhead, it felt cool and airy.

Although the wagons creaked and rumbled louder than any forest sounds, Ruth was just beginning to think she could hear a gurgle of water when a shout went up from the front of the wagon train.

Knowing one can't really quicken the pace of an oxen

team, Ruth and Mariah grabbed their younger sisters' hands and tried overtaking the wagon ahead of them. The track only narrowly cut through the underbrush, however, and having heard plenty of warnings about small children slipping under the iron-rimmed wheels, the girls decided not to risk it. Instead they had to wait until the wagons in front all drew up in the clearing.

The clearing was new, with greenery just poking up through the blackened ground where the underbrush had been burned away. On the far side stood a small sturdy log house, its squared-off logs still raw and white. Uncle Joe's horse was tied to a sapling near the east wall.

Leaving the wagons and their teams, the travelers made their way across the clearing, drawn to the solitary cabin. They talked excitedly to one another and laughed out loud, eager to see this Promised Land for themselves. The girls' feet grew black as they scuffed across the charred ground, which provoked giggling until they realized that the rest of the group had quieted.

The women slowed their steps, pulling at their husbands' shirtsleeves to draw them back as well. Aunt Almeda, leading Robert in one hand and Lizzie in the other, soon was the only person still approaching the house. Just as she glanced over her shoulder and realized she was alone, Uncle Joe stepped around the corner, grinning from ear to ear.

"Mrs. Naper, welcome to your new home," he said, holding out his hand. Almeda smiled back, just touching her bonnet brim in one of those coquettish gestures she brought from the east before placing her slim fingers in his square palm. He led her around the corner to the front of the house.

When snow still covered the ground, Uncle Joe had stood on that very spot and charged Mr. Scott to build the house right there. Every settler preferred to build his home so that the single door opened on the south, useful for catching daylight and for telling time. By a lucky coincidence of the landscape, the south side perched on a ridge that sloped gently down to the river, offering a broad vista of greenery with sparkling water beyond.

The other families gathered in the small yard while Aunt Almeda inspected her house. Small and empty as it was, the inspection didn't take long before they were back outside. Granny Naper went in for a look with Sally Ann and Aunt Betsy, while some of the others explored down to the river with Uncle Joe to discuss the sawmill.

The girls propped their wildflower bouquets against the wall as a housewarming gift, and Ruth and Mariah peered in the doorway to admire the new house. A puncheon floor instead of dirt! A little splintery still, but that would smooth down

Puncheon Floor

A floor made of logs split lengthwise. The round side lay on the dirt with the flatter part turned up as the floor.

soon enough. And you could hardly see any specks of daylight through the shingled roof!

When they came back out of the cabin, one of the women was talking with Aunt Almeda. She threw a glance over Almeda's shoulder at the little house with the blackened field beyond. "Nothing like Buffalo, is it?" she sighed.

Almeda's eyes were fixed beyond the woman in front of her, tracing where the forest rolled down to the river and up again on the other side in gentle green swells flowing out to the horizon. "No, nothing like Buffalo," she smiled quietly. "Which is why we're here."

Ruth heard excited voices from below offering different opinions on where the sawmill should be built and speculating on how soon it would be up and running. Another lively discussion reviewed the talents of each settler. Who was best suited to design the building? Which of them had a knack to install the iron machinery?

So much depended now on the settlers doing their part and pulling together to make the community successful. Hard work awaited them all. "And with no applause," Ruth thought, smiling to herself. Only their own satisfaction in a job well done.

Daidi and Mother stood close together on the bank, a little off to one side. They faced downriver, their voices eager and their eyes animated. Ruth slowly made her way over to join them, pondering the roles people played in their communities and in their families.

"Well, Cailín, what do you think of your new home?" Daidí asked.

Ruth shook off her deep reflections. "We're not all going to live with Uncle Joe, are we?"

"Until we build our own house, we'll probably stay nearby," he answered. "But your Mother and I are thinking we might backtrack a bit along the river. I'll take Ned and scout out a site just as pretty as this for *my* bride!"

Mother colored. "Go on with you!"

A sudden squeal from Cordelia made Ruth spin around. Coming down the bank from the cabin, Cordelia had tripped on a root. Dirt streaked her pinafore and her face puckered up as if she were about to cry. Gran teetered just a few steps above her on the steep slope.

"You shouldn't go running down the hill like that!" Gran scolded. "Wait for Ruth to come help us. Ruth! Ruth!" she called.

Daidí turned to Ruth, a meaningful look in his eye. "Sounds like you're needed, Cailín."

The confusion in Ruth's mind suddenly cleared. Her place in the community, her importance to her family, her talents, her

Pinafore
A sleeveless dress or apron worn over a girl's dress to protect it from dirt.

185

gifts—everything came into focus. Ruth threw a smile over her shoulder at Daidí as she ran lightly along the shore and up the hill to where her grandmother and sister waited for her.

"It's a little slippery here, Gran. Take my arm," Ruth said. Ruth held out the other hand for Cordelia and helped them both down the slope where they joined the rest of the settlers on the banks of the DuPage River.

THE DUPAGE RIVER AT LAST

THE PIONEERS

Founder of Naperville:
Joseph Naper, *age 33*
His wife: Almeda Landon, *age 31*
Their children:
    Robert, *age 6*
    Elizabeth, *age 3*
    Maria, *age 1*

Joseph's brother:
John Nelson Naper, *age 31*
His wife: Betsy Elizabeth Goff, *age 23*
Their children:
    George Austin H, *age 4*
    Jay H., *age 2*

Joseph's sister:
Amy Anna Naper, *age 38*
Her husband: John Murray, *age 46*
Their children:
    Robert Nelson, *age 16*
    Ruth Eliza, *age 12*
    Amos H., *age 8*

Cordelia Maria, *age 6*
Sarah Ann Murray, *age 20*
Her husband: Henry Babbitt, *age 21*
Their child:
> Eunice, *age 1*

Joseph's, John's and Amy's mother:
Sarah Hawley Naper, *age 64*

Neighbors from Ohio:

Harry Wilson, *age 34*
Orra, *age 30*
Their children:
> George, *age unknown*
> Aurelia, *age unknown*
> Perhaps 3 others

Dexter Graves, *age 42*
Olive Graves, *age 40*
Their children:
> Loring, *age 17*
> Louisa, *age 16*
> Henry, *age 10*
> Lucy, *age 5*

Sarah Ann Murray Babbitt's in-laws:
David Babbitt, *age 43*
Eunice Babbitt, *age 49*
Their children:
    Lucy, *age 15*
    Eunice, *age 13*
    David, *age 9*
    Solomon, *age 7*

Neighbors from New York:

Holder Sisson, *age 41*
Clarissa Bronson, *age 38*
Their children:
    Allen, *age 14*
    Anna Mariah, *age 10*
    Harriet, *age 7*
    Eleanor, *age 5*
    Clarissa, *age 1*
    Susan E., *born 1831*

Philip F.W. Peck, *age 22*

Lyman Butterfield, *age 34*
Amanda Hooper, *age 25*
Their children:
    Mary Neeley, *age 16?*
    George W., *age 11*

Almira, *age 4*
Andrew Jackson, *age 3*

Harry Boardman, *age 39?*
Lovina, *age unknown*
Their children:
    Horace, *age 12*
    Adaline, *age 10*
    Sabra, *age 5*
    Charles, *born in July*

Robert Strong, *age 25*
Caroline Willey, *age unknown*

Selah Lanfer, *age 32*
Mary Knapp, *age 31*

Orrin Stevens
Sophie Derbyshire

Origins Unknown:

Ira Carpenter, *age unknown*

(Possibly William) Bond, *age unknown*

Although new babies, marriages and unexpected deaths would rearrange them in the coming years, the above information is a snapshot of the families in July of 1831. At publishing time, this information was as accurate as possible. New facts will certainly surface in the future to give us a fuller picture of these founding families.

Chronology

The actual dates of the journey vary depending on who is telling the story. The registered owners of the *Telegraph* were John Naper, Joseph Naper, and Reuben B. Hickox. While the enrollment record says John lives in Ashtabula, Ohio, Joseph is listed as being "of Dunkirk, New York."

Logically then, if this was Joseph's expedition, it must have started in Dunkirk. P.F.W. Peck says he left Buffalo, New York on June 1, 1831. (History of Chicago, Bross) Henry T. Wilson reports he left Ashtabula in June, (Portrait and Biographical Record of DuPage County) although Henry Graves thought they left the last of May. (Sunday Chronicle)

When they arrived in Fort Dearborn is also imperfectly documented. Peck remembers a two-month trip, which would make it late July. The Graves' family monument states they arrived in Chicago on July 15, while Robert Nelson Murray thought he was in DuPage by July 17. (Portrait and Biographical Record of DuPage County)

A recorded fact, however, is that Joseph Naper's name is removed as a listed owner of the *Telegraph* when the ship is re-enrolled on July 13, 1831. Traditional history states that Joseph sailed the ship to Illinois, selling it on arrival, which the enrollment record seems to support.

For the purposes of the narrative, I chose to have the *Telegraph* leave Buffalo during the evening of May 31, 1831. Henry Graves figured it was a week later when the ship docked in Detroit and they decided to take a wagon the rest of the way, which would be approximately June 7. Assuming Joseph sold the *Telegraph* on July 13 after the voyage to Fort Dearborn was complete, the settlers could easily have arrived at the settlement site by July 17, just like Robert Nelson remembered.

For dates during the rest of the journey, I researched the ports that were in operation in 1831. I decided which ones the *Telegraph* would likely have stopped at and how long they might have remained. I learned about the difficulties in crossing the St. Clair Flats, the prevailing winds on Lake Michigan, and the calming effect overnight when creating the *Telegraph*'s itinerary. According to shipping records, spring was cool and wet that year, and the ice on the lakes broke up later than usual. Finally, many of the *Telegraph*'s passengers, especially the Graves family, remember the voyage as being particularly stormy, so that became an important part of the story.

Resources

"American History 1800–1860: History Online Sections" Conner Prairie
www.connerprairie.org/historyonline/1800.aspx

Currey, J. Seymour. Chicago, its history and its builders: a century of marvelous growth Chicago: S.J. Clark Pub. Co., 1912.

Danckers, Ulrich and Meredith, Jane. A compendium of the early history of Chicago to the year 1835 when the Indians left. River Forest, IL: Early Chicago, Inc., 1999.

Tocqueville, Alexis de. Democracy in America. 1805–1859. Chicago: University of Chicago Press, 2000.

Whitman, Narcissa. "Diaries and Journals of Narcissa Whitman 1836." The Oregon Trail.
www.isu.edu/~trinmich//00.ar.whitman1.html

Moore, Jean. DuPage at 150. West Chicago, IL: West Chicago Printing Company, 1989.

Thompson, Richard. DuPage Roots. Wheaton, IL: DuPage County Historical Society, 1985.

Anonymous. Early Chicago: reception to the settlers of Chicago prior to 1840, by the Calumet Club, of Chicago, Tuesday evening, May 27, 1879. Chicago: Calumet Club, 1879.

Anonymous. Early Chicago and Illinois. Chicago: Fergus Print. Co., 1890.

Johnson, John W. "Family History". Lawton, IA: J. W. Johnson, 1928.

Moore, Jean. From Tower to Tower: a History of Wheaton, Illinois. Wheaton: Gary-Wheaton Bank, 1974.

Anonymous. Genealogical and biographical record of Will County, Illinois: containing biographies of well-known citizens of the past and present. Chicago: Biographical Pub. Co., 1900.

Graves, John Card. Genealogy of the Graves Family in America. Buffalo: Baker, Jones & Co., 1896.

Anonymous. Historical Encyclopedia of Illinois. Chicago: Munsell Pub. Co., 1909.

RESOURCES

Bateman, N. & Shelby, P. Historical Encyclopedia & History of Kendall County, Illinois, Chicago: Munsell Publishing Co., 1914.

Williams, William W. History of Ashtabula Co., Ohio. Philadelphia, Williams Bros., 1878.

Large, Moina W. History of Ashtabula County Ohio. Topeka-Indianapolis: Historical Publishing Company, 1924.

Andreas, A. T. History of Chicago from the Earliest Period to the Present Time in three volumes. Chicago: A. T. Andreas, 1884.

Bross, William. History of Chicago: historical and commercial statistics, sketches, facts and figures republished from the "Daily Democratic press"; What I remember of early Chicago: a lecture, delivered in McCormick's Hall, January 23, 1876 (Tribune, January 24th). Chicago: Jansen, McClurg & Co., 1876.

Anonymous. History of Cook County, Illinois: being a general survey of Cook County history including a condensed history of Chicago and special account of districts outside the city limits, from the earliest settlement to the present time. Chicago: The Goodspeed Historical Association, 1909.

Richmond, C. W. and Vallette, H. F. A history of the County of DuPage, Illinois: containing an account of its early settlement and present advantages, a separate history of the several towns, including notices of religious organizations, education, agriculture and manufactures, with the names and some account of the first settlers in each township, and much valuable statistical information. Naperville: Caroline Martin Mitchell Museum, Naperville Heritage Society, 1974.

Blanchard, Rufus, History of DuPage County, Illinois. Chicago: O.L. Baskin & Co., 1882.

Mansfield, J. B.. History of the Great Lakes, Volume I. Chicago: J. H. Beers & Co., 1899. Lewis, Walter and Baillod, Brendon. A transcription for the Maritime History of the Great Lakes site. Canada: Maritime History of the Great Lakes, 2003. www.halinet.on.ca/GreatLakes/Documents/HGL/default .asp?ID=s027.

Anonymous. The History of Will County, Illinois : containing a history of the county, its cities, towns, &c., a directory of its real estate owners, portraits of early settlers and prominent men, general and local statistics, map of Will County, history of Illinois illustrated, history of the Northwest illustrated, Constitution of the United States, miscellaneous matters, &c., &c. Chicago: W. Le Baron, Jr. & Co., 1878.

Luzerne, Frank. The lost city! Drama of the fire fiend, or, Chicago, as it was, and as it is! And its glorious future! : a vivid and truthful picture of all of interest connected with the destruction of Chicago and the terrible fires of the great North-west: startling, thrilling incidents, frightful scenes, hair-breadth escapes, individual heroism, self-sacrifices, personal anecdotes, &c., together with a history of Chicago from its origin, statistics of the great fires of the world, &c. New York: Wells & Co., 1872.

Gale, Edwin O. Reminiscences of early Chicago and vicinity. Chicago: F.H. Revell Co., 1902.

Anonymous. "Loved Horses and Sport." Sunday Chronicle 5 April 1896.

Lewis, Walter. Maritime History of Great Lakes. www.hhpl.on.ca/GreatLakes/HomePort.asp

Karamanski, Theodore J. Schooner Passage: sailing ships and the Lake Michigan frontier. Detroit: Wayne State University Press, in association with the Chicago Maritime Society, 2000.

Anonymous. <u>Portrait and Biographical Record of DuPage and Cook Counties</u>. Chicago: Lake City Pub. Co., 1894.

Towsley, Genevieve. <u>A view of historic Naperville from the skylines: a collection of articles of historic significance</u>. Naperville Sun, [1990], 1975.

Schmidt, Leone. <u>When Democrats Ruled DuPage</u>. Warrenville, IL: L. Schmidt. 1989.

Moore, Jean. <u>Young People's Story of DuPage County</u>. Dundee, IL: Crossroads, 1981.